THE SACRED CONTRACT

Book II

The Accounts
of a Pleiadian Traveler

Nakala Akasie

Point of Light Pleiadian Publishing

© 2015 Nakala Akasie All rights reserved.
www.whenangelsspeaktous.com

(sc)ISBN: 978-1-942445-00-5
(e) ISBN: 978-1-942445-01-2

Library of Congress Control Number: 2015937908

Printed in the United States of America
10 9 8 7 6 5 4 3 2 1

Editor: Aaron Rose
Cover designer: Ana Inacio
Typographer: Marsha Slomowitz
eBook: Marcia Breece

ACKNOWLEDGEMENTS

It is by design of the powers that be that this
book came into existence. For me it is impossible
to individually name all of the people and beings of light
who contributed to this work. I would like each of you
to know that it is with great consideration and
gratitude that I hold you in my heart.

~*Forever*, Nakala

CONTENTS

INTRODUCTION

By Nakala Akasie

I now understand that I am a Pleiadian traveler. I have journeyed far from my land, the star system of Pleiades, from my own people…my family… in order to experience something new, something magical. That is, to live on this great Earth with a great diversity of people to learn about their cultures, their values, and their beliefs. To put it plainly, there is a vast mixture of ideas that the people here create that I wanted to be a part of, to experience and learn from.

You can see this place, the Pleiades, if you look up into the sky on a clear night. There is the star system of the Pleiades among trillions of other bright shining stars. Some of the people call the Pleiades the *Seven Sisters.* Perhaps this might assist you in remembering and finding this place where I came from and call home.

Many people never ponder their origins…perhaps never had reason to. I did.

It has been six years since a group of light beings came to me and began to speak to me; through me, even. Here it is called channeling. They said they were the Akasie, a group from the Pleiades—my family who had come to assist me throughout my journey.

I couldn't see these beings with my physical eyes but I could sense where they stood and I could feel their energy and hear their words. I knew they were with me, and I knew they loved me in a way no one on this Earth ever has.

I was full of questions. I wanted to know who these great beings were who could talk to me without anyone else hearing. I wanted to know why they were here. I wanted to know why they had chosen me.

A being who introduced himself as Quem instructed me to write down all the transmissions—every message that I received from the beings of light. He also directed me to journal everything—my interactions and the feelings associated with them as well. He told me that we would be sharing the messages that I received with the people of the Earth.

To be honest, what was happening scared me because my life was changing—my world—the way I looked at things. I have been comfortable with the beliefs that have been drilled in me by society. Now, all of that is changing. I am realizing that some of the ways I perceive things aren't for my highest good. Nor are they for the highest good for humanity. In essence, I have been living an intricately woven life of mistruths that I was about to unravel.

Often the truth, like a tiny snowflake, is hidden in the shadows until the light breaks through. Unless you look very closely, you will not see the true design—what has been there all along.

In a way it is all very peculiar…the way we are born here on this Earth in a tiny body of flesh that, given the correct conditions, will grow into a magnificent person who has the ability to create and experience anything the mind can conceive.

As a small child I learned to obey…not to examine…not to explore and be a free thinker. I went to school, just like all the other kids. There, they told us to sit at a desk for hours to learn what *they* believed to be true, what was important for us to know. They molded us into a particular pattern—a particular way of thinking. Little did we know they were programing us to be a specific way to fit into a manageable box created long ago that has little to do with who we truly are—how we were individually created to express ourselves in that God-given way that makes our hearts sing.

To my great fortune, I have awakened to my true reason, my true purpose for coming to this great Earth. I am a traveler. I am here for the journey…the experience. I am here to feel my heart sing.

~Nakala

PART
ONE

MASTER QUEM ARRIVES

CHAPTER
ONE

It happened suddenly and with tremendous force—the sound was like thunder crashing in my mind. There was a flash of light so brilliant that I was momentarily blinded. I heard myself utter a profanity followed by "Oh, Dear God." I took a step back away from the light. It did not help. The entire room was still lit up. *Is this what it was like when the atom bomb went off?*

I felt my body tremble and my legs go weak. Without turning my head, I reached behind me for something solid to support my body, but I felt nothing. I waited for the noise to stop. It was incredibly loud, and the light was hurting my eyes. I felt my body respond to the surge of energy. My eyes were closed, yet I could still see the light—brilliant and all-consuming. Unconsciously, I tried to make myself small and inconspicuous. I'll never know for sure how long I stood there…I felt like I was a ghost, frozen in time.

Then, all at once, the noise stopped. My mind cleared and my thoughts began to formulate with such an immeasurable speed and fluidity that I thought perhaps I had stepped out of this world into another one, from which I was able to access information that I had never before even known existed.

Several years back, I had experienced a similar event. It had been Master Quem, (Kw-Ah-m) who had come to visit me and allow me to see him in form. Since then, we had communicated telepathically. I wondered if this was Quem again. I wondered if it was possible. It was all so fantastic. *I must be dreaming,* I thought.

When I finally was able to force myself to open my eyes, I saw a translucent vapor, like a rolling cloud of fog. It was comprised of a rainbow of colors that swelled and undulated. The vapor seemed to be alive and breathing of its own accord. I stood there transfixed, my attention focused on the extraordinary colors and movement. A thought crept to the forefront of my mind: *If I look away—even for a second—this energy may disappear.*

Then, all at once the colors of the vapor began to take on a more tangible form. They slowly moved together and melded. The colors flowed so easily, so gracefully together. It was as if there was a gentle breeze coaxing them to move this particular way.

Out of the corner of my eye, I caught sight of a movement just to my left. I saw a form beginning to take shape. Instinctively, I knew that this form would continue to evolve, eventually taking the form of a person—just like it had the last time. I was fascinated and full of anticipation as I waited for whoever (or whatever) this was to fully materialize. I so hoped that it was Quem.

All at once I felt my body shudder, and I realized that I had locked my knees and was holding my breath. Beads of perspiration had begun to form on my brow and in between my breasts—wetness began to roll down the center of my chest and lower back. Nervously, I wiped my body and felt heat rising up from my skin. A familiar flush spread across my chest and neck. I moved my hand to the nape of my neck and felt my hair—it was damp. I wanted this *thing* to get on with it…make itself known, whatever it was. Slowly, deliberately, I inhaled as much oxygen as I possibly could into my lungs before I exhaled. The last thing I wanted to do was faint!

Never once did I take my eyes off the sight before me. The colors were more vivid now and had begun to swirl with more intensity. A momentum of energy was building, like the pressure does when a storm is brewing. Feeling like I may get sucked in somehow, I instinctively took another step back to find the wall for support, thinking that somehow this would protect me.

Coming from nowhere, a gentle breeze moved over my body and I felt a damp chill take hold of me.

For years I have been channeling messages from different light beings—mostly from the Pleiadians. Others had come as well to communicate, but to see the energy take on form like that…that was an entirely different matter.

Again, I drew in another long breath. What I saw before me was amazing. Consciously, I knew that I was totally safe, yet I felt an underlying apprehension in my body; it was tense and rigid. I was afraid. I knew that what I was witnessing was beyond all reason.

A feeling of being paralyzed overtook me. A buzzing in my ears began—just like it had before. *I was entranced, yet I wanted it to stop! I wanted to feel normal again. Why was this happening to me?*

I saw two distinct energies. With one, the colors seemed to deepen slightly and merge even more. *What was it?*

The other vapor was like a fog or cloud, but transparent. I saw the form of a man begin to take shape. Was it the same being who visited me before? Was this Quem, my spirit guide?

✳ ✳ ✳

The first time Quem appeared to me, he said that he was from a star system called the Pleiades—a nation far away from Earth. A part of me thought I had lost my mind, while another part was excited to have this connection.

Quem had spoken to me in great length about his nation, the Pleiades; he wanted me to understand that he was a dignitary and a peacemaker. He was a member of the Galactic Federation. Quem, alongside many of his brothers and sisters, had traveled here freely to assist the people.

The group that he was from, the Akasie (Ah-Kas-ee), has stood back for many eons, waiting for the time when certain people of the world would begin to stir from their slumber to remember and understand that there are many life forms and intelligences from the higher realms or dimensions waiting for the time to reveal themselves. They have waited for us to ask and accept their assistance in going forward in a multitude of areas.

Quem went on further to explain that I was a matrix of cosmic energy—a soul that had taken the opportunity to inhabit a physical body like I had so many times before on this planet, which he referred to so fondly as our Mother Earth. He went on to explain that we as a people were here to evolve—to learn to love on a deeper level, unconditionally.

✳ ✳ ✳

Both clouds of vapor began to evolve and disintegrate. I could see clearly that it was indeed Quem. As he stepped forward toward me, I felt a wave of love envelop me. I breathed in the energy like it was my favorite perfume; I wanted it…him…to remain forever.

Questions began to surface with incredible speed. There was so much I wanted to know and to learn. *Why was he here? Why had he chosen to reveal himself this way?* For Quem to appear to me here, like this, indicated something significant—something very special.

Very slowly, he raised his arms up toward me as if he wanted to embrace me, but neither of us moved toward the other. There was a white, vaporous substance pouring from his hands—he was directing this vapor toward me. I knew he was calming me down; I instantly felt the anxiety I was holding in the pit of my stomach subside.

Suddenly, I focused my attention on my journal. No words were spoken between us, but I knew Quem wanted me to go to the adjoining room to get it (and a pencil) so that I could record his message. I hesitated for a moment. *If I leave the room, he may not be here when I return. Again, I wondered if this was just a lucid dream.*

Finally I obeyed, and when I returned to the living room, I saw that Quem was now leisurely standing by the window. His gaze was fixed on my back yard. He turned toward me and in a hushed tone said, "Your friends appreciate your kindness." Quem was referring to the birds that were feasting at the feeders in the trees near the house.

Quem moved to stand before me and patiently waited until I was ready to receive his message. I headed straight to my overstuffed chair and reached to turn on the antique brass lamp next to it. I sat down, and my attention instantly shifted to the way my body felt on the chair. I loved the look and feel of the soft, blue fabric and the way the chair seemed to accept my weight and love me. I pulled my legs into lotus position and opened my journal to the next available blank page. I automatically checked the tip of my pencil and shook it to make sure that there was plenty of lead in the cartridge. I quickly wrote down the date and who was giving the message and then I looked up and nodded to Quem that I was ready to begin.

Quem continued to stand, as he began to speak in a soothing tone. "I have for you a wealth of information. However, I must not exceed your ability to receive. You are like a delicate flower, and must be cared for as such. You are to follow my guidance in the coming days—this will serve many purposes."

I listened carefully to Quem's words. At times, his manner of speaking confused me. I focused all of my attention on his words so that I would understand his true meaning.

Quem continued, "It is your time to fully understand why you have chosen this incarnation—this life stream." He smiled knowingly as he extended his hand toward me. Quem was watching me, assessing my energy; he knew that I was beginning to feel anxious. I felt a peace overtake and subdue me—it was unlike anything I had ever felt before. My entire body was tingling and vibrating, and in the midst of it all, I felt love, serenity, and a great appreciation for this gift.

My fears dissolved in an instant and my mind and body relaxed completely—I felt the weight of my world leave me. I had no choice but to close my eyes; I felt my head drop to the side like I was going to sleep. I knew Quem was putting me into a deep state of relaxation. I still could think clearly and wanted to test what was happening to me, so I commanded myself to open my eyes and lift my head, but I was unable to make my body respond. I did not have the ability to do anything other than listen to Quem's words. My full focus was on his voice and his words—the sounds of the outside world completely disappeared.

Quem began by saying, "Today marks specific," *[Editor's Note: Throughout the book, we have preserved Quem's unique way of saying things. In this case, he means, "Today is a special occasion ...]* "as I have come to you as my witness to reveal certain information that will assist you throughout your many steps, taking you forward on your path—your life's purpose."

Just for an instant, in his voice, I heard a hint of sadness. I had heard the story before, but he wanted to tell me more about our relationship and why I felt such a deep connection to him; this Oneness. He continued, "You are my daughter, born of the origin of the Pleiades. Your mother, Sarah, allowed me to give you the name Cathryn long ago. The memories are in your cells, and when you are near me those memories are awakened—alive with a knowing that is certain and fixed." Every time Quem spoke of our relationship using the name Cathryn, I felt a deep longing, while my vibration rose considerably. To me, this indicated that I resonated with the information; I knew without a doubt that what he said was true.

Quem continued on, "It has been many months since I have revealed myself in this way to you. However, I have continued my communications somewhat during this time. There have been many other beings from other star nations as well who have, shall we say, kept you in their sights. Your gift to receive communications from the higher realms is not by happenstance. You were selected, and you agreed upon the task at hand.

"Now, in turn, you are to record all of our messages and all of your interactions with family and friends. In general, you are to record all activities, individual and shared, of seeming importance. There are many reasons for my instruction."

He paused for a moment and allowed me to absorb not only his words but also the sun's warmth that radiated through the nearby window. I felt my gratitude swell.

My attention was drawn to the quiet…the stillness. I waited for Quem to continue speaking, but he did not. Through my eyelids I saw the color red. For some unexplained reason I opened my eyes. I realized that I was no longer under his magic spell. The communications had stopped. I found myself once again aware of my surroundings and able to move my body with ease. I thought it was strange that Quem would suddenly stop speaking. *What was going on?*

Quem stood near me with his hands outstretched; he looked directly at me and I saw in his eyes a deep pool of peace and understanding. He knew of my insecurities and fears. I did not hear his words, but we were communicating. I felt the emotion and the knowledge that told me that he was well aware of all that I was experiencing. Somehow he was conveying to me that everything would work itself out if I would allow him to direct my steps.

My attention shifted. Quem was now standing near the window. I wondered why he had not chosen to sit down. Perhaps he was being polite and was waiting for me to ask him if he'd like a chair. However, that thought vanished as quickly as it had come.

I began to make notes of what he looked like and what he was wearing. If one did not look closely, Quem could have easily passed for an ordinary man on the street, if one didn't look into his eyes or notice his unusual dress. He wore what looked to be a white linen robe, but not of a familiar sort at all. The cloth had a quality to it that seemed to create an iridescent sheen—luminescent. But maybe it wasn't the cloth itself that glowed. Maybe it was Quem's aura that was glowing through and around the cloth!

The robe hung almost to the floor and had a noble flair to it which implied that the man who wore it was of great importance. It was designed to be very loose fitting, flowing freely with every movement. The fabric draped off Quem's shoulders in pleats down to his waistline. To keep it all in place, he wore a purple sash that looked to be about five inches wide. It, too, was pleated. The fabric that was used to accent the v-neckline was the same royal purple that was used for the edging for the kimono-style sleeves. The purple was deep and rich—a hue that was used in the courts of kings.

For a moment, I looked away from Quem and toward a swirling fog that had appeared; I was lost in thought. With a deep breath, I felt a rush of energy rise in my body. So beautiful it was.

Suddenly, out of the corner of my eye, I noticed tiny sparkles that flashed over by Quem. *What was happening now?* Turning to get a better view, I looked directly at Quem's robe and saw tiny bits of metallic gold thread that had been embroidered down the pleats on the front of the robe. *Was it this gold thread that had pulled me back?*

I really did not want to stare, but in order to see the detail I had to look closely. On the purple edging was more of the embroidery. The thread was so tiny and delicate that I had almost not noticed it. Someone had taken great care to make this garment for Quem. There wasn't any sort of fasteners like zippers, snaps, or buttons that I could see. He wore what appeared to be simple brown leather sandals but of a fine quality.

What really caught my eye was the large emerald gemstone pendant that hung around Quem's neck from a bold gold chain. The gemstone was refracting the light from so many directions—it was simply stunning!

The gold chain the gemstone hung from was crafted with alternating gold discs connected by little jump rings, also gold. The discs were approximately ½ inch in diameter. Each disc had some sort of ancient symbol etched on it.

The emerald had a faceted hexagonal cut and was brilliant in color and clarity and set in a gold filigree bezel. The piece looked ancient, but retained its beauty, nonetheless. The size of the stone was impressive, and as near as I could tell it was well over one inch in diameter and lay precisely over his heart. Quem had worn the same necklace the last time I had seen him.

Quem's skin was white, with a healthy glow to it, like he spent a fair amount of time outdoors. For a moment, my mind drifted to the possible activities that he might be involved in, before I made note of his hair. I had never seen anyone who had hair this white before. His hair had a nice wave to it, with lots of body.

As I looked again at Quem's shoulder-length hair, I noticed that Quem had a light around him. Maybe that was why his hair looked so white. He had a full beard, also pure white. His eyes were a soft blue that pulled me in deep. From my perspective, his features weren't particularly striking or unusual. It was his eyes and his overall manner that held me captive.

The style of Quem's clothing, except for the pendant, reminded me of what Jesus may have worn on a day he went to temple over two thousand years ago.

From where I sat, I could detect that Quem was average height (about six feet tall) and build. He wasn't a big man that commanded physical power, his power came from within. Again, I glanced at Quem's eyes and was transfixed by his quiet strength. He merely waited for me to finish my study.

Overall, his presence was of someone of great authority, and I felt that he carefully weighed all of his options before he took a step in any direction.

I felt so comfortable with Quem that I had forgotten to voice any of my questions. They had simply vanished from my mind. I worked to retrieve them. Nothing came.

Quem remained quiet for some time. The energy to his side remained, but the intensity of the movement had calmed somewhat.

Remaining seated, I surrendered to the energy of love and let my mind wander.

From the work that I have been doing with some of the beings who frequent my home, I have grown accustomed to unusual things that happen to me. Sometimes my home feels like a hub where the guides come and go. Nathanal (Nuh-than-al), my personal guide, has explained to me that the beings will often stay in my home for days or even weeks at a time and then travel somewhere else to assist others. Often I have no knowledge that they are even in the same room as me.

Quem has been the only being that I have been allowed to see with my physical eyes. Sometimes I sense their presence—I just know they are around me.

Then there are the ones who like to announce their arrival by making noises—thumps in the walls or loud pops in my refrigerator. Perhaps they do not want to hang around unnoticed, but wish to get on with their reason for being here. Maybe they are in a hurry and have somewhere they must go, so they let me know they are here.

I suppose it is much like a telephone call. If I don't answer the call, they disconnect and go do something else. Maybe they will call again. Maybe they won't.

Then there are those who come and don't say a single word, but my body picks up their energy. My vibration goes higher and I feel the unmistakable emotion of love—serenity.

Suddenly, I heard a movement…a rustling sound…and I was drawn back from my thoughts. Quem had turned and was walking into the kitchen. He felt my gaze and turned around to address my question that was never verbalized. "I am going to make you a cup of tea just now. Jasmine is it? Stay where you are for a moment and relax. I'll be back directly."

Quem's movements were slow and deliberate, like there was nothing more important than this moment. He seemed to be completely at home. I smiled as I thought about a Pleiadian serving me like this. I heard the cabinet door open and the sounds of him being perfectly at ease in my kitchen. I chuckled under my breath. Quem is in my kitchen, making *me* tea?

I realized that I felt strange, like I really wasn't in my body. Pulling an afghan over my lap, I relaxed somewhat. My mind began to drift again, back in time to when I was married.

Everything had changed since the Pleiadians came to work with me. Everything. I was no longer married. I had moved away. I lived alone… well, sort of.

Quem returned as he promised, carrying a tray with my red ceramic teapot and cup, a cloth napkin, and also a few cookies to the coffee table. Carefully, Quem set the tray down and went to the couch across from where I sat and sat down.

With no prior indication, he bowed his head and began to pray. He was giving thanks to God for this opportunity to serve the people of this world who suffered from the sense of separation from Him and their true essence.

He went on to thank all of those who had agreed to come here to this world to assist in the great awaking and work to further evolution, taking all into the Light of God. I felt my love swell as I listened to his voice and felt his reverence for all of life. He ended his prayer by saying Amen.

Quem slowly lifted his head and looked straight into my eyes in a way that revealed a kindness and love that I recognized as pure. He was watching me very closely and listening to my every thought, waiting for an opportunity to begin to speak. He chose first to address his appearance, specifically the gemstone he wore. With his fingertip he lightly touched the stone as he said, "The emerald is of great import to the Akasie, my family—your family.

"All Akasie members of higher authority wear this ornamentation for purpose of identification. In addition, the emerald serves as a communicator. It vibrates at a particular octave, which assists us with many functions.

"As for my dress, and this includes all Akasie members, we wear what is functional and in accordance with our endeavor. All fibers are natural and support us being for the highest good."

Suddenly, my awareness shifted to what was happening outside. The wind had picked up in strength and there was a tremendous downpour of rain, followed by a loud cracking noise and then a terrible thud. There had been a beautiful sky only moments before, and now? Something sizable had fallen. However, at that moment I didn't feel the need to get up from my chair to see what.

✳ ✳ ✳

Unexpectedly, I was taken back in time to when I was a young child, not more than seven or eight years of age, living in Kansas. (I knew that Quem was assisting me to remember something of great significance in order to heal something.)

There had been a Brownie meeting (Girl Scouts) after school. While I was at the meeting there had been a terrible storm. The winds had been fierce and the rain had poured down in torrents. The house didn't have a basement, so the leader took us all into her small kitchen during the worst of it. She had turned on a portable radio to hear the weather reports.

How I got home I have no recollection, but upon my arrival I saw that our front yard, from the street up to front steps of the house, was nearly half covered in water! We had a large ditch that ran parallel to the street. To have more rain than the ditch could handle was a rare occurrence indeed.

As children, we didn't miss those kinds of opportunities. When a good rain came we'd make a run for it to get our swimsuits on and go play in the water. On this particular occasion, I wanted to do just that or maybe get my bicycle out and ride through the water on the driveway. But for some reason, thoughts of my rabbits out behind my house had arisen, overcoming those childhood fancies.

My objective was to see if my rabbits were okay. As a young child, I was given the responsibility of caring for a few cats, one dog, and several rabbits. My job was to make sure they had food and water every morning before school and every evening when I got home.

Some mornings the temperature was well below freezing. Oh, how I hated going out on those days! My skin would quickly turn a numbing red. Back then, little girls wore cotton dresses; our legs were bare— exposed to the elements. But that made no difference to anyone. I was expected to do my job. After the rabbits were fed and watered I had to walk to school. The extreme cold made a lasting impression on me.

Many times the water in the rabbit's crocks would be frozen solid, so I had to carry each crock back to the house, knock the ice out, and refill it with fresh water. Some days it took me a good while to do this process, as I had to make several trips back and forth. The area was some distance from the house.

On the day of the storm, instead of playing in the water with the other children on my street, I chose to turn in the other direction and run as fast as I could to the back of our brick home where the rabbit hutches were. When I arrived, what I saw shocked me. All the cages had been knocked over! Fearing the worst, I slowed down as I got closer. My mind raced ahead with graphic images of dead rabbit bodies all mangled, bloody, and stiff in their cages.

How could they possibly survive?

We had a family in one of the cages—a mama and her eight babies, all of them with jet black fur. It wasn't unusual for them to have big families. I could see them clearly in my mind. They were so soft and cute. They were nearing the time when we would have to find new homes for them or build more cages.

Instead of seeing what I expected, though, I saw that some of the doors were flung open. I slowly looked in each cage. Feelings of being helpless and afraid surfaced.

The first rabbit cage was Thumper's. He was white, big, and mean. When he was agitated he would hit the cage with his back feet and make a terrible racket, hence he had earned the name Thumper. As usual, he sat in the corner of his cage. There wasn't any blood that I could see. To me he looked okay. He was one rabbit I didn't dare mess with, so I quickly went to the next cage.

When I looked in the next cage for the family, I saw just the mother. She was huddled in the corner of her cage with the door open wide. She seemed frightened but unharmed.

None of her babies were there! As quickly as I could, I shut the door to the cage. I sank down to my knees in the soft, moist grass. I guess I must have sat there for a few moments.

My imagination rolled into high gear as I envisioned those babies being thrown out of their cage and being carried off by the wind to God knows where. I was afraid to look around to find their little bodies lying broken in the grass. I loved my rabbits above all else.

Every one of the cages had been knocked over on its side. I was a young child and not strong enough to pick up the cages, and I wondered how I would get them back into their rightful positions.

✳ ✳ ✳

I paused for a moment and wondered why this particular memory had emerged. A question crept into my mind: *What was Quem going to show me?*

⁎ ⁎ ⁎

It had all happened so quickly. I didn't know what to do, but as I sat there I saw movement to my right. I turned my head to find two of the bunnies in the tall weeds under a nearby tree at the corner of our lot. A few more feet and they would be on the other side of the fence in our neighbor's yard. I panicked. They were eating, their little black noses wiggling as they chewed the tender leaves.

They didn't seem to have a care in the world. With my fingers, I felt the lush green grass and marveled at the moist, soft texture and took in a deep breath.

It seemed we saw each other in the same instant, and my sadness turned into a mixture of happiness that in a split second shifted back to fear. They were too close to the fence. If they hopped just another two feet I wouldn't be able to get them back.

In one swift movement I was up, making my way toward them, but I had to be careful that I didn't frighten them. As I got closer I saw more bunnies, and to my delight, some of the bunnies began to hop toward me. I counted them. All eight were there. Would I be able to get them back into the cage before they decided to go off in the other direction? Once they got going it would be difficult, if not impossible, to get them back.

The bunnies had never been out of their cage all at one time. I knew what I faced. Could I get them safely back into their cage where they lived with their mother? I scooped one up after another, holding each briefly— loving it while feeling its soft jet-black fur before returning it home. Why, they weren't even wet or upset! They seem to be asking me, "Where have you been?"

⁎ ⁎ ⁎

Again, I questioned. Why did that particular childhood memory surface at this precise moment? How odd, I thought.

⁎ ⁎ ⁎

As the story unfolded, I could clearly see the images as if I were actually there, reliving the experience once again. In addition, I felt the same emotions flooding my being of fear, sadness, happiness, and a fantastic weight of responsibility.

How amazing, I thought, that I, at such a young age, would feel so responsible for these creatures. As I thought on it, I wondered where my parents were during that incident and why I hadn't gone to get their help.

A sound brought me back from my reverie. I saw it was Quem. His robe rustled as he shifted to make himself more comfortable.

His feet were clearly in my view and then came this absurd thought in my mind: "Why, he has feet just like an ordinary man." Then I remembered his ability to read thoughts. My face was blazing with embarrassment as I whispered, "Oh God." I heard myself sigh heavily. I knew he had heard me. He *always* hears my thoughts. The only thing I could do was apologize for being insensitive and comparing him to an ordinary man—ordinary was not even close.

Quem merely smiled knowingly and dismissed the whole thing without saying a word.

What was he doing? I waited for some sort of sign that would indicate his direction. Watching closely, I saw his chest expand. Yes, he was breathing just like he had a physical body. Oh, God! I did it again. I knew that my face was crimson by now. Taking a chance, I looked at Quem's face. Would I be able to tell if he had caught my thought? Nervously, I shifted my body. I was growing more uncomfortable as the moments ticked by.

Quem didn't change his posture. He merely looked at me. I couldn't read his expression. Then he suddenly smiled. His teeth were white and even. All at once he laughed out loud and his entire body shook.

Finally I began to relax, figuring that he must have experienced this sort of thing countless times before. I let out a sigh of relief and laughed at myself. The embarrassment was gone. In his own unique way, he had reassured me that there would be no harsh words nor any sort of reprimand.

What happened next threw me off guard. He somehow shifted my gaze across the room to a framed picture. It was a hand-colored lithograph of a simple English cottage in the country. The large picture hung on the wall to my right from where I sat. As if this were an everyday occurrence, Quem instructed me, "Watch carefully. I want to show you something."

Turning to get a better view, I scanned the picture carefully and took note of all the details. The picture was matted in a navy blue silk mat with a ½ inch white margin surrounding the image, which provided a great contrast so I could see more easily. My logical mind took over and I wondered why Quem was showing me this picture. Maybe the lithograph had slipped, making the margin off kilter.

Without warning I suddenly began to see the image easily lift up and slide sideways outside of the white boundary, overlapping the top of the navy mat. I blinked several times with disbelief and awe. All I could manage to say was "Wow."

How Quem had managed to move the image like that was a complete mystery to me. I sat there and thought about it. I knew of no logical explanation. Perhaps it was an optical illusion. Still…

"My desire was to get your attention there," Quem explained. "I suspect I did just that. You are being gifted. Know it. With my assistance, you are being allowed to see some things that defy your third dimensional reality."

As if he were directing my thoughts, the loud wind and the noises of something falling earlier popped into the forefront of my mind. I began to contemplate—to stew over what had happened. There were no prior warnings about a storm coming through this area. My concern grew of probable damage to my property, and I felt that I should get up and see to it. Even so, I felt that I may be rude in doing so. I looked to Quem for a signal to tell me that it was fine for me to check it out. He only nodded his head once as if to say "Yes."

CHAPTER
TWO

How long had I sat there in the chair? My legs were a bit stiff. Carefully, I moved my legs out from under me onto the floor. Slowly, I stood up and waited for my body to tell me it was time to take a step.

Walking over to the window, I caught my first glimpse of the lawn that was heavily littered with leaves, twigs, and some smaller branches—I felt the pressure build of having more work piled on me. I was reminded that I had no one to turn to for help in situations like this. Then I noticed how the sun was being reflected in thousands, if not millions, of tiny rain droplets that lingered on the grass and other vegetation. They glistened and shimmered. How beautiful!

At first, I didn't notice anything of significance that would have made such an ugly noise. Continuing to scan the yard, I finally found the object of my concern in the far corner of my yard. A very large branch from the maple tree had broken and fallen.

My opinion was that the branch had been literally ripped off of the trunk, and all for no good reason. I felt a surge of remorse and then a stab of anger well up as I thought of this innocent tree losing a limb…to what? The wind! What right did the wind have to cause such havoc? I loved that tree. It was a beauty.

I was sure that the action had left a splintered, gaping wound in the tree that would literally take years to heal over completely. How sad for the tree to have to deal with the stress of it all!

Next, I noticed how close the branch had come to hitting my fence. I estimated the size of the fallen branch to be about fifteen feet in length. In my mind's eye, I saw the damage that might have been done had the branch fallen just a little further to the west.

What a relief to not have to deal with all of the details of making a claim on my insurance. I stood by the window for a few moments longer, surveying my property. I didn't see any more damage, but still I felt a sense of loss for all of it.

As I turned around, I caught Quem's eye. All along, I realized, he had been quietly observing me. His eyes reflected my feelings of contemplation and loss when he began to speak again.

"The storm was for a purpose. The tree branch, unfortunately…the structure was weak and because of this, let go of its true purpose."

"It's true purpose?" I pondered out loud.

"Yes, the tree branch was part of a whole, a network if you will, all serving one purpose, and that was to express itself in a particular manner. This particular branch simply wasn't strong enough to survive the powerful cleansing winds. I speak of the connective tissue. For some, the pressure is too great to hold on to their true purpose."

I worked his words through my mind and for some reason felt compelled to begin to voice what I knew about trees, which was precious little. "I suppose a tree expresses itself by giving. Other than that, I really don't know anything about trees. I do love them, as they give color, form, and dimension to our world. Would you please explain your comment?"

He went on to say, "A tree is one of God's many spectacular creations and comes to the third dimension to live his or her life out by serving his master, just as you do. It is the choice of the tree, just as it is your choice, to live here in this world.

"The energy of a tree is spirit fulfilling his or her desire to be of service by providing oxygen (the air that you breathe from the trees with the process of photosynthesis). A tree serves in a multitude of ways by providing its body, or what you call wood, for unlimited tools, paper products, trinkets, and structures of all kinds. In some societies wood is used for fuel to heat homes and for cooking purposes. Remember, the tree's canopy provides protection from the elements for many living creatures.

"Some of the trees give over their lives to assist those who walk the Earth and know that this is their ultimate purpose."

Quem went on to say, "The tree is God's creation and is a living creature with intelligence and emotion. The maple tree has lost one of his limbs, and for this we grieve."

In the next breath, Quem added, "The tree will survive, and as the wound heals he will grow even stronger. The tree learns, just as you do, from his experiences.

"The tree served today in a very profound way by allowing us to use his body as an example or gift. Simply put, we have been allowed to use this experience as a lesson for you—a way for you to awaken a childhood memory. That experience as a whole assisted in shaping your life as you know it. You were taught at a very young age to be responsible for those under your charge.

"Do you remember, Nakala, that you were to share the responsibility of caring for the animals with your older brother?"

Inwardly, I groaned and immediately wanted him to stop talking about this. Instantly, I saw Quem's motive—his purpose for taking me back in time. I knew that Quem was working to teach me, and through this teaching, ultimately, I would gain a great insight and be able to heal and move on.

Quem chose not to address my thoughts, but instead continued on, "However, on many occasions your brother's choice was to not care for the rabbits.

"His oversight, be it out of forgetfulness or pure neglect, both angered you and saddened you. On a conscious level, you do not remember the times you voiced your concern to your own mother and even your brother. There was no mistake in the message you received—nothing changed. Your concerns about the rabbits going hungry made no difference. The rabbits still went uncared for, time and time again.

"I go on…It wasn't just your rabbits that depend on humans to protect them and treat them fairly; every living creature requires fair treatment—equality—and certainly this means to be loved. In essence, the message you received was, "You didn't matter enough to be heard, nor did the rabbits matter enough to be cared for." In your young mind you saw that the rabbits weren't being treated fairly and neither were you! I sum it up quickly here: You were not important or worthy enough in the family unit for your parents to uphold the rules and make sure all abided by them."

The memory was painful and I had quietly begun to sob. My heart ached. Even though decades had passed, I remember well what happened. The pain I felt remained strong, intact. I was distraught that those animals were allowed to be treated that way, so I had taken it upon myself to take on the responsibility to do my job as well as my brothers.

I hesitated for a moment and then blurted out in anger, "Why are you here? Why are you bringing up these memories in me?"

My vision blurred and the tears spilled over, down my cheeks and onto the pages of my journal. For some reason the memory haunted, even tormented me in the very core of my being. I also felt embarrassed to show my feelings in front of Quem. I am a grown woman who has raised my own family, but with this memory the hurt was unleashed and I felt like an unprotected child once again.

What was being presented brought back a rawness inside of me that ached deeply. I felt it and I finally understood that I had been angry all of these years. But that wasn't the whole of it. I knew there were deep wounds left in me, similar to the tree's, that I needed to learn from—that needed to be healed.

Ten years ago when my brother suddenly passed from his body, the only emotion I felt was anger. I was angry that he had left his wife and four young children. That day or any day that has followed, I have shed not one tear on his behalf. Always, I have known from my inability to feel remorse that there was something incredibly wrong, although I wasn't able to identify what.

Then the realization hit me hard! Oh my God! My brother had done it again! By his death, he had avoided fulfilling his responsibilities. I was in judgment of my brother; I had resented him all this time!

Quem took me from my thoughts by stating, "My purpose here is multifaceted. I am a traveler from the far-away nation of the Pleiades who has come to assist you and others like you who are ready to move forward and begin the healing process. I am your teacher and I am your father. You are my Cathryn, whom I love and have always guided throughout your many sojourns here in this world and other worlds as well.

"You have come to live out this incarnation in a physical body, and you require guidance. You are a student, and to be successful in life you are to have a teacher, a master. Because I love you, I have taken it upon myself to be that teacher—that master. It is my pleasure to do this. Because I have chosen this path, I have chosen you as *my* responsibility, just as you chose to be responsible for those rabbits many years ago. You took care of them because you loved them, not because you had to. You see the correlation?"

Quem is a strong teacher, and I saw the wisdom of his words. "My purpose is to assist you in the reawakening of memories that will undoubtedly assist you in the healing process. The memories allow you the opportunity to revisit times during your life that have set forth a pattern or created certain beliefs that have kept you imprisoned.

"The time has arrived when you are to assess your lifestyle and your beliefs and reinvent yourself." Quem spoke in such a matter of fact way that I felt totally at ease. For some reason, I just knew that what he was saying was correct.

Once again, Quem expertly changed the subject. I listened intently, as I have learned that everything that is said by one of these masters is never idle chitchat but a lesson on some level.

Quem began talking about the energy that had manifested earlier—the colors that I had seen in the vaporous substance. "The energy that you saw just previous to my arrival was given as a gift to you. The energy was imbued with colors that correspond with the seven chakras and the seven-fold flame.

"Everything has a tone or vibration; this includes what you saw prior to my arrival. This was given to you to assist you in opening your awareness to a higher level—to activate you. In other words, what you experienced was a specific frequency opening up particular pathways in your brain in order for you to receive my communications in this way. The activation was to increase your vibration to a much higher level.

"Next time I come to your side, please go within and know that this is a grand gift to you and in turn a grand gift to all of creation, as all that you receive is received by your counterparts—all intelligences and life forms everywhere and always. All energy reverberates outward. Accept my gift, please, with love."

Quem continued on with his teaching, "I have come to you for many reasons, as I have stated before. One, my aim is to assist you in your healing process by releasing cellular memory that has held you back.

"Two, my purpose is to teach you how to replace those miscreations with new beliefs that allow you to love yourself and in turn love all others unconditionally.

"Three, I am here to serve all of mankind through my service to you."

Throughout his speech, I worked to make my notes as I watched him intently. His mannerisms fascinated me. I wanted him to tell me more about the Pleiades and the Akasie.

However, over time I had learned that when I had asked for personal information, my guides either don't like to talk about themselves or that is simply not their priority. Usually, they would expertly shift the conversation in order to teach me something. This had been done so many times that I had come to expect their finesse. Whatever the case had been, I felt like it would be interesting to learn about the culture of the Pleiades and the family of Akasie.

Quem heard my thoughts and said quietly, "I am your father, and I only want what is best for you. Time is of the essence. We are at the peak of the cycle when you are most motivated to make changes in the way you think, feel, speak, and act. We use particular situations and life events to teach you.

"Our mission is to assist you on your soul's path. Part of what we do is to assist you in healing, and this may take on many forms. Never do we work to avoid or sidestep your questions.

"However, our main goal is to work to retrain you to think positively and remain in the now. To *Be* in this moment is of utmost importance.

"We see you at times sway precariously from one thought to another. Thoughts instantly create emotion. You carry yourself as if the load is so very heavy, not knowing the way to uplift or balance yourself in fullness. At this moment, to teach you to balance is our main objective."

Quem sighed as if he, too, were tired or somehow troubled. It occurred to me that maybe he needed rest. Then I formulated my question. "Do the beings of light sleep like we do?" I looked up into his eyes, and just for a split second I thought I saw that he carried a heavy load himself.

"I have been patient for your return home. Many lifetimes have passed since you have paid even a short visit. As your father, I will say this: I grow weary of the many things that you have placed your attention upon that are merely distractions and have no real bearing on your spiritual growth.

"We, as your family, see now that you are ready to not only listen but create disciplines that will bring yourself back in alignment with the Cosmic Divine Creative Awareness—God." He was correct; I was ready to listen and work on myself.

"As your father, I give instruction and delegate to those in our group, the Akasie, who are qualified *and* willing to teach you. You have met many of these teachers already. One way they work with you is by connecting you to people who can assist you in your steps forward. We are very careful who we connect you with. Know that with each person, there is always at least one valuable message that is meant to assist you in your journey back to God.

"The communications you receive are much like a plate of food given to you. My instruction is to carefully assess what is given to you. Listen to the words—feel the intent behind the words. Much of the words are nothing more than fluff made to stroke the ego or fill silence. When you compare a plate heavily laden with food meant to appeal to the senses with communications, you can see quite clearly that not all may be as it seems, nor for your highest good.

"As you look upon your overloaded plate of food, all of your senses are invoked, sometimes even to the point of being overloaded. There, before you, are vibrant colors, textures, and aromas, and lastly the tastes.

"You see that to partake of all may cause you to become uncomfortable to the point of becoming ill. You simply do not require all that is before you.

"This is exactly the same with exchanges between people. You must discern what pieces of the message are useful and which are not—take what you can use and leave the rest behind.

"Quite possibly you may want to go back again to the same source when you feel you are ready to partake again.

"What I tell you is quite valuable. There are times when people take in too much information. Of course, in these situations you cause an overload, and most of what you receive is lost, simply because you are unable to process it for your highest good. I am sure you have experienced what I speak of, yes?"

Quem did not wait for my answer. He continued on, "For this reason, you have not gained from the real message, which is meant to carry you forward on your journey. Quite possibly, you don't even recognize there was a message! Thus you must receive once again the same message or information in another manner until you do get it. I caution you to go slowly and allow yourself the proper time to work through each message to receive it in fullness.

"Up until this point I have kept very close watch over you, my daughter, and have given you many teachings. I see you excel in many areas, while in other areas I have seen you flounder. The time has come for you to realize that you are interpreting some of the messages you have received from us.

"I speak specifically about some of the people we have connected you with. At this time I won't go any further with this subject."

Part of me wondered, why not? I really could use some guidance. But then another part of me was grateful to not receive any more information. All of this was getting to be a little much.

Going back to what I had seen and felt concerning the rabbits, I wondered if I didn't understand the entire lesson yet. I had reacted so strongly to what I saw and felt that I knew there was something I wasn't seeing or understanding that had to be important—useful.

As if I had spoken out loud, I heard Quem remind me, "Yes, this is one of your lessons, and for this moment you have received the information necessary for you to process and learn your lesson." He paused for effect, then continued on. "Already you feel as if I am moving too fast for you to understand what I have presented thus far. It is most wise for you to back up to the first scenario."

Quem shifted his position. With his movement, I was reminded that I could use a break. I wanted to get some fresh tea and asked him if he would care to have any. He politely refused.

Getting up, I felt stiffness in my legs. I had been sitting for some time and really did need to move. As I made my way into the kitchen, I noticed that the cloud of energy was gone. I wondered if Quem would ever explain to me how that was created and by whom?

The teapot was sitting on the stove-top, already full of water, so I turned the heat on high and reached into the cabinet beside the stove and found the bag of loose green tea, a clean tea ball, and a tea cup.

I wondered about the caffeine in the green tea. With a twinge of guilt, I thought about Quem watching me drink tea full of caffeine.

Turning to see where Quem was, I was surprised to find him leaning in a relaxed way on the doorjamb that joined the living room with the kitchen, calmly watching me. He certainly was discreet. He was watching me move about in my kitchen and no doubt listening to my thoughts that I kept forgetting were being broadcasted into the ethers.

I thought, well, here we go again. Nervously, I tried to cover up my thoughts and feelings of guilt with a worthwhile conversation and began with, "You know, I am utterly confused about this caffeine thing. Some people say it is good for you to have a few cups of coffee a day, while others interject that caffeine alters the brain chemistry and is addictive and is something that would be good to avoid. Quem, what is a person to do these days with all of the controversy concerning our food and drink?"

Quem simply chuckled and smiled before he gave me an answer. "Nakala, remember our first lesson? We will get to the issue of caffeine a little later."

The water was ready. I went to get the teapot and poured the hot water in my cup. My stomach growled. I really was a bit hungry but thought eating in front of my guest a bit troubling. Grabbing a bag of raw almonds, I politely held it out for Quem, knowing he would probably refuse my offer, but I did it anyway. He shook his head no. I went ahead and took a handful for myself to nibble on while we talked.

After both of us had found our seats in the living room, Quem waited patiently while I ate my almonds and drank a bit of tea. As I drank my tea, I made a note that the flavor of the tea was exceptionally smooth. So many times I allowed the tea to brew too long, causing it to become bitter. I sighed with satisfaction.

My next thought was that this sure was rude of me, to drink and eat in front of Quem.

Of course Quem heard me, and this time he decided he was going to make a comment. He took a deep breath before he began. "Nakala, my diet is a bit different than yours. My body would not benefit from the types of beverages and foods you partake in. You see?"

In the past, I had always suspected something was different with the way the guides sustained their bodies in comparison to us. I mean, how could it not be different? They had bodies that we in the third dimension aren't even able to see unless they want us to.

I wanted to know how they maintained their bodies. Subsequently, on different occasions, I had tried different angles to coax a few of my guides to talk about the subject. Specifically, I'd ask what they ate and when. So far I hadn't had much success in getting any of them to speak on the matter.

Even though Quem's statement had been rhetorical, I took it as an opening for further discussion, and I wanted to take advantage of it. "No, I don't see how the foods I eat would not benefit you."

There was a definite gleam in Quem's eyes. Evidently, nothing gets past him.

Quem moved his hands upward toward me once again, and I felt a calm wash over me. "Nakala," his tone sounded reassuring and a bit mesmerizing, "I'd like to give you a bit of advice. There is nothing you cannot ask me outright, although I always weigh my options before I forge ahead with any answer. This time is no different.

"We are both made of the same stuff. The difference is that I allow the sacred cosmic energy directly from Source, which is from our God, to flow through my body untainted."

I had heard a little about how we as humans qualify energy with negativity by going into judgment. Which to me equates to the fear we create over just about everything, i.e., will I have enough money to pay my bills this month? Am I going to find my soul mate? If I do, will I recognize him? My car has been acting strange, am I going to have to put in more money to get it fixed? But I wondered, how do these thoughts affect the diet?

Again, Quem heard my questions and spoke so softly that I barely heard him. "My dear Nakala, by allowing the Divine Cosmic energy of love to flow freely through us, we have gained freedom from the lower, denser energies. Because of this, our vibration, or the rate that our atoms vibrate, is much faster. If we choose to eat, our diets must be pure in quality (nothing processed, and all the freshest and highest nutrition possible). Because of this, our need to replenish is less frequent, if at all. It is the same with our sleep patterns. We simply do not require the constant replenishment that you in the Earth bodies do.

"Sweetheart, by allowing the light to shine through you more and more, you, too, will see a change in your diet and sleep. This all is inevitable and comes about quite naturally when you let go of the fear that has overcome every move in your daily life. You think I exaggerate? No! The negative thoughts continue on at a subtle level, with you left unaware."

Just then I heard a rumbling noise that sounded like it could be coming from anywhere, but as I listened more closely I knew it was coming from somewhere behind me. I couldn't imagine what was happening. The noise reminded me of a long, slow, rolling thunder, but I knew it couldn't be thunder. The sound came from inside the house and was low and steady in pitch.

Turning so I could see behind me, I looked closely for any subtle or not so subtle energy in the general direction of the far corner of the living area. I thought I had pinpointed the sound near my fichus tree.

The sound didn't diminish at first. I saw nothing there that could cause such an unusual noise. My stomach tightened as I waited for something more to happen.

Finally, I turned to Quem and gave him a questioning look. Neither of us attempted to say anything. He just nodded and motioned to the area in the far corner to my left side and behind me.

I continued to stare at the corner, waiting for what, I didn't know. Anxiety had made its way home in my gut. Suddenly, as quickly as the noise began, it stopped. Now, it was so quiet that I could have heard a pin drop.

I was on high alert and almost in a state of panic. Nothing was being said or done to ease my anxiety. Nothing.

Quem sat perched on the couch like all was well. I looked at him and searched his facial expression for some sort of clue to tell me what was going on.

Quem clearly could tell what I was feeling and on what level. He merely waited until I caught myself and began to breathe deeply to regain my balance. I asked myself, "What else could possibly happen?"

After I had regained my self-control, Quem politely asked, "Why were you concerned? I am sitting right here in the same room and I assure you that nothing harmful will come about. You are completely safe."

He went on, "Being in a human body is a tricky business. You have an internal mechanism or switch that comes on when you encounter something out of the ordinary. It is meant to get you to react in the case of danger—to save the physical vehicle. Simply put, you have a warning system that has been set in place to assure that the human race continues on.

"Your system is working quite well. When you encounter something like you just did, your instinct is to run for cover. However, in this particular instance, you did not. You sat here feeling the signals, but you ignored them. What would you have done had I not been here?" Dumbfounded, I just sat there asking myself that very question.

After a few moments of contemplation I answered him. "Honestly, I do not know. What was that sound? Did you do that?"

Quem didn't miss a beat. "There are others about who are assisting with your lessons at this time. Do not concern yourself with it. The purpose of the sound was to instill the emotion of fear." Nice of you, I thought.

"We must go back to the rabbits. During that particular storm, you not only heard the horrendous winds but *felt* the terrific pressures that moved the house until it groaned. You saw the sky turn to a muddy yellow as it let loose its horrific power. For you and your friends, it was made into a terrifying experience. Because of this, you pushed it down into the recesses of your memory. I ask you now, do you remember the storm?" I had to confess to him that I had very little recollection of that time.

"When something that significant happens, it will leave its mark upon you. More accurately, the fear created in your emotional body is felt on the physical level. Unless this emotion is expressed or released in an appropriate manner, it will remain in the cellular structure.

"When you feel fear, be it obscure or not, you feel threatened. Your instinct is to either freeze to make yourself invisible or run away as far as humanly possible.

"There are many situations in which fear is brought forth and on many levels. This particular time, you were afraid for your life. The storm was wild and unpredictable. Anything could have happened. The home you were meeting at could have been easily swept away. *You* could have been swept away. This was clearly understood by you at the time and most certainly provoked the emotion of fear.

"When the situation of caring for your sweet rabbits came about, you were faced with the issues of equality and repression. The subsequent emotions were created."

Disrespectfully, I interrupted Quem just then by saying, "Wait! We were just kids. Kids will avoid doing their jobs. Things like that happen all the time. It wasn't all that bad."

"Look at it closely before you defend the actions of another, or even yourself. At first glance, when we examine the situation of caring for your rabbits, the emotion of fear is overlooked, because in this case the emotion was felt on a subtle level. Are you able to readily recognize the emotion of anger because of unfair treatment during that time?"

I answered him quickly, and without meaning to I allowed the anger to rise and spill over. "Well, of course I recognize that I was angry. I still am! I am pretty sure you know that I am angry."

Surprised and embarrassed at my childish outburst, I shrank back in my chair. I saw how expertly and quickly Quem was able to provoke me. Even so, I didn't see any shift in Quem's demeanor. He remained poised as he went on with his teaching. "Well, of course I know you are angry to this day over the inconsistences of those particular childhood rearing practices. The reason I asked you this question was that I wanted to bring forth the full measure of anger if you were able. I'd say I accomplished what I set out to do."

Shaking my head in disbelief, I heard myself mutter almost inaudibly, "You *wanted* to make me angry."

In a gesture of deep respect, Quem slowly bowed his head, giving me a single nod, acknowledging that he had indeed heard me before he continued. "To work through a memory like that, you must be able to understand your true feelings concerning it. There are others who, if given the very same set of circumstances that I have given you, would not be able to tell me they feel any emotion at all, even though the anger precariously simmers under the surface, ready to erupt at any moment, much like a volcano that boils and spits to release the volatile pressure in its belly. Do you see?"

He went on, "Even though a person may not be able to identify an emotion of this sort, there are usually, if not always, physical symptoms that give away buried feelings such as anxiety, which promote symptoms like tightness in the abdomen and/or chest, shallow breathing, or even holding your breath. Occasionally, there may be sudden outbursts of anger from little or no provocation. Undoubtedly, sooner or later the denser energies like anger and fear will come forth, dear one."

Quem's voice was very soothing, but still I was feeling sick to my stomach. He paused before he continued on, "Inequality and tyranny are two huge ways to suppress and control people. These behaviors begin in the home or community." Briefly, I wondered where he was going with this.

"Think of your Civil War. Slavery was behind that one, was it not? Some of the slaves—not all, mind you—were held in captivity and chains and forced to work in unspeakable conditions. If they didn't comply with their master, they often were stripped and whipped."

I interrupted again. I was agitated. I felt he was blowing this thing way out of proportion. I had lost control and was unable to make myself sit any longer and listen to his speech. "Quem, please! The differences are vast here between my having taken on the chores concerning the rabbits because someone else wouldn't and the cause of the Civil War!"

Still Quem showed no display of emotion. "Ah, you think my choice of comparison is that different? The difference lies only in the measure of severity of the action.

"I'd like you to look at those rabbits. They were held captive and treated unfairly by many—specifically your family, and before your family there were others. I am not only speaking of not being fed but of being held captive in a cage, unable to move about freely to forage for food as they desired and to live their lives as they wanted to! They depended on your family for their survival. These rabbits had never been free to graze in the fields unafraid.

"On some level, even as a young girl, you understood this. You certainly understood the concept of being fair. Not being treated fairly is a threat to your survival.

"What you don't understand, my dear Nakala, is that it all comes down to the law of life. Treat others as you want to be treated.

"You may not have understood this on a conscious level, especially as a child, but these fears that have been provoked in you time and time again have created layer after layer of a protective shell, if you will.

"These fears come from first-hand experiences, such as the storm discussed previously, or from second-hand information, such as stories about storms (or any other event that may be construed as negative) told by people, viewed on television, or in other types of media coverage, such as newspapers or programs.

"The shell I speak of is a dense energy created from thought and feeling that has been allowed to take residence in first your mental, emotional, and etheric bodies and then lastly manifesting in your physical body.

"This energy is dense and over time may be given to blocking the physical tissue and organs, preventing an optimal flow of life energy. This is how illness, disease, and death of the physical body will manifest itself.

"In addition, you have inherited from your ancestors their memories that are stored in the DNA and your own memories from hundreds, if not thousands, of past lives as well!

My mind was racing to sift through the information being given to me and apply it toward my life. But what kept creeping up was the questions, "What is in it for you? What do you get out of teaching me? Why not just let me go?"

While I was thinking of those questions, I knew that it was my ego that was fighting to maintain the same belief systems I have had since I was a child and probably before that—the belief that I was not worthy to have another assist me.

At that point, I got up and said, "Excuse me, please," and walked to the window. I stood there for some time, just wanting to be held and told that I was safe.

CHAPTER
THREE

After some time, I turned to Quem and said, "Quem, I feel like I am really messed up. I have believed all along that I don't measure up. How can I change this?"

I felt the heat of my body overtake me, and I wondered what was happening. "Why do I feel that awful heat?"

Patiently, Quem responded to my plea, "Breathe deeply and raise your vibration. The heat is your body working to correct the negative energy that you are creating."

I took several deep breaths, letting go of doubt and the need to know all the answers in this moment. As I breathed, I noticed the heat began to dissipate.

"Nakala, we are working with you on many levels to reveal to you areas that require your attention. You have work to do here in this dimension, as well as in other dimensions. But we now desire to talk about the work that you are to do while living on the Earth at this time."

Again, I paused to think on the implications of what Quem was saying before I asked, "What work? I thought it was clear-cut that I was to do channeled readings and teachings and write the material that you instructed of me.

"What else have you got for me? My life is already full—*very full*. How else can I serve and still have time for myself?"

Quem looked me straight in my eyes and held my gaze. I felt the depth of his love pouring from him through me and I began to cry.

"Nakala," Quem began, "I am assisting you in the release of negative energy that has taken residence in your body through many layers of sadness, grief, and so on. When you feel the love emanate from me or another from the higher realms it moves your energy—emotion—thus allowing the dense energy to be released. When you experience this, I ask you to stop and recognize this as a beautiful gift and give thanks for it.

"This allows you to fill that space that we have created with love. This teaches you to love with a higher level of awareness or consciousness.

"Ah, Nakala, I have waited for such a long time for you to ask to receive assistance from the higher realms: the angels, the masters, and your very own spiritual guides!"

I had noticed that Quem had begun to use my name Nakala and I felt a pang of melancholy that he had stopped calling me by the name Cathryn. Intellectually, I understood that perhaps it was best to move on, but still Cathryn was like a pet name and it felt good for him to acknowledge me as his daughter in this way.

I was still wallowing in the murky pools of self-pity when I heard Quem's voice. "It has been two years since I asked you to make the formal and legal change from your birth name on this plane to Nakala Maria Angelic Akasie.

"At that time I explained to you that to change your name was an outward expression of your commitment to serve humanity. You were frightened to make the change for several reasons. I bring this up now because the name change still brings forth fear. You on the lower level of consciousness have not realized this."

Quem took a deep breath and expelled it slowly before he went on. "The steps to change your name were extensive, to say the least. The legalities were tedious and stressful, lasting for many months to complete. But what is the most difficult for you to accept is the fact that many of your friends and family members still refuse to acknowledge this new name change. If they will not comply with your new identity, step away from them."

My mouth dropped open and I shook my head in utter disbelief. "You're serious?" I was in shock. I could not manage another thought. *How could Quem ask this of me?*

There are so many friends that I love dearly, even family members, that tell me they cannot use my new name. They say, "We have known you by the name Jackie all of your life. It just doesn't feel right to call you Nakala."

Quem paused before continuing on. "Nakala, out of respect these people are to honor your wishes. If they are unable to honor this gift that has been highly bestowed upon you, then simply you are to move away.

"Every time your old name is used by one of your family members or friends, negative energy is created—your thoughts and emotions, Miss, are what I speak of. You feel like you must defend yourself and your new name…you feel put against the wall. You feel pain because these people refuse to see and acknowledge the new you.

"Nakala, what we have seen you do is make excuses by responding like this: 'Oh, I don't mind if you continue to call me by my old name.' Miss! The fact is, you do mind! That old name holds a frequency, a lower vibration. We ask that you move into the new frequency in totality. This new name is a gift to you, and I ask you to accept it in fullness."

The heat rose in my face. I was embarrassed to admit that yes, I did feel like this. I heard myself say, "You *are* serious," only this time I felt like I was resigning to the idea. At the same time, I understood his meaning. A weight and a pressure to act began to build inside of me. I didn't like the implications of all of this.

Then a distinct memory surfaced. A friend of my mother's told me (in front of my mother, no less, and in no uncertain terms) that I was being disrespectful to my parents by changing my name.

I shook my head again, knowing full well what I was being told to do. "But how on Earth do I move forward with this?"

Quem smiled and nodded his head. "What you do, dear Nakala, is address the issue every time it comes up by explaining that you have taken on a new name as an outward expression of your dedication to serve God by working as a channel. The name Nakala reflects that expression. If the person is of the level of awareness to understand the concept of vibrations or perhaps ready to learn about this concept, by all means go on and explain how everything is energy and everything vibrates. We are moving to a higher vibration now. The name reflects this shift.

"The name Nakala, simply put, is a higher frequency than Jackie. The name Nakala reflects your new vibration. Ask them to please understand this and honor your wishes. I believe this will open their eyes a bit and most assuredly will touch their hearts."

Unexpectedly, Quem announced, "Nakala, I must bid you my farewell for today. I will come for you tomorrow at 3 p.m. if you are available to receive."

Quem stood up and smoothed the creases from his robe. He looked at me again and I felt peace wash over me. What I said next took me by surprise. "Father, I will be waiting for you."

✳ ✳ ✳

After Quem slowly faded from my sight, I continued to sit and rest, allowing myself to reflect on what had just happened. My pencil was still in my hand and my journal still sat in my lap.

During our time together I had recorded as much of what was said that was possible without losing my focus on the conversation and Quem. There were undoubtedly large gaping holes in my writing, and the sooner I edited the work the better.

I thought of the enormous job ahead of me. I knew that if I didn't get it down I'd lose valuable pieces of information. There was much here to absorb and process, and the best way I knew how was to write it out and feel it all again. Simply put, tomorrow Quem would return and expand on his teachings. My aim was to be ready.

But first, I decided to take a much needed break, so I went to bathroom, pulled off my clothes, and got in the shower, letting the steaming hot water stream over and down my body. I hadn't realized how tense I had become. Umm, it felt good to relax. After I dried off, I quickly got dressed and headed into the kitchen to find some dinner.

There wasn't any possible way for me to accurately estimate how long it would take me to go through the material I had received, but I was sure it would take several hours of writing. I wanted to be well fed and comfortable before I settled down for the evening.

As I passed through the kitchen, I saw the cookie jar on the counter and automatically headed toward it and lifted the lid. I reached inside the jar and grabbed a handful of cookies before I caught myself. This is what I do when I get too hungry—go for the quickest, but not necessarily the best, thing. Oh, Perfect!

To my dismay, the analogy about the food and communication came to the surface of my mind. The statement "Only take what is for your highest good and only as much as you can process at a time" had made its mark.

Looking down at the cookies in my hand I thought, no, perhaps I should find something a bit healthier. Maybe a salad would be better. Putting back the cookies didn't shift my craving at all. If anything, my cravings grew stronger, and I felt a strong sense of disappointment—I had wanted a quick fix.

Focusing on what was in the refrigerator, I began to pull out all of the salad fixings I could find and prepare a nice, healthy salad that I knew would satisfy me.

After dinner, I made some tea. Not one cup, but an entire pot of jasmine tea, and then I went to the computer. I sat down and opened my journal to rewrite everything and add more detail as I went. As I wrote, my emotions resurfaced. I felt like I was one of those pendulums swinging from one extreme to another. I was spent, and I knew I should just quit and go to bed.

But when I got into bed, I just lay there, as the images and conversations replayed in my head again and again. I wondered how I had gotten to this place in my life. The gratitude swelled and the tears fell from my eyes, landing with tiny plops on my pillow.

Suddenly, it occurred to me that Nathanal had been silent for many hours and none of the other guides I work with had spoken to me, either. It is a rare occasion when that happens. I had been totally absorbed in rewriting the information that I had received earlier. Obviously, I had needed quiet time to get through my work. I whispered, "Thank you for this time, guys."

Nathanal, politely said, "You're welcome, my dearest Nakala."

Even though I was quite comfortable, I laid there for quite a while. Sleep wasn't coming. My mind refused to settle down. Then I began to contemplate what would happen tomorrow when Quem arrived.

Finally, I asked who was around, hoping to engage someone in a conversation. Usually there are at least two guides with me, and sometimes

I have had as many as five or six around, for whatever reason. There is never a time when I am alone.

Before I had a chance to verbalize my question, I suddenly found myself in a sitting position in my bed. I turned on my light and sat there and began to pray for guidance. I knew that I wanted to change—to stop sliding into the past or looking into the future. All this ever accomplishes is anxiety that keeps building. Heck, I was there right now, worrying about what would happen tomorrow when Quem came back to speak with me.

When I finished my prayer, I asked, "Nathanal who else is here with us?"

Nathanal responded by saying, "Now isn't the time, Nakala. It is your sleep time. Turn off the light and empty your mind of thought. It would be wise if you were rested tomorrow when you receive your father."

I felt a hot tear slip out and fall down my cheek. "Nathanal," I began, "I need help. How am I going to do what I have been asked to do? I feel so tired. Please help me."

Nathanal quickly reminded me, "Nakala, you know that Rome was not built in a day, nor will these teachings be integrated by you in a day. You will continue to receive lessons over your lifetime. Please do not fret over what has been given to you or what the future may bring."

I had to laugh, then. Nathanal had used the Rome analogy many times before to get me to lighten up and know that I was feeling sorry for myself.

Nathanal continued to speak in a comforting voice. "You are to stay in this moment only. Breathe. Let your anxiety lift, and remember that as long as you remain here in this very moment, you are always free. I love you, Missy."

CHAPTER
FOUR

I woke up to the sun's light streaming through my window. So inviting it was. Then, like a jolt of electricity, I remembered the previous day and the implications of what today may bring. Quem would arrive this afternoon. It wasn't long before I realized that I had to stay focused on my task at hand or my day would be unbearably long.

After I had a glass of warm lemon water, I walked into my office. First, I lit a white candle in celebration of a new day and out of respect for the beings of light that work with me, and I found some music to play while I prayed and then went into meditation.

However, this morning my stomach felt queasy. I knew I was nervous about my meeting. I wanted to move—to get busy so I would focus on something other than that meeting! So I hurried through my meditation and headed to the kitchen to begin cleaning up. I wanted to make sure the house was tidy before my company arrived.

Quickly, I finished my chores. The clock read 11:30 a.m. My thoughts kept jumping to my meeting with Quem. I felt like a child, nervous and excited at the same time. My stomach continued to feel like it had a bunch of butterflies in it.

Repeatedly, I found myself looking at the clock and calculating how much longer it would be before Quem would show up.

The weather looked inviting so I decided to venture outdoors and assess the tree limb situation up close. The limb had fallen merely inches from the fence.

I stepped out onto the grass in my bare feet and was surprised at how cold the wet grass was from yesterday's rain. I almost wanted to turn around and go back into the house, but curiosity pulled me out to the fence. I wanted a closer look at the maple tree.

As I got closer to the tree, I began to see plainly that the branch was bigger than I had first estimated. There was no way that I could handle the cleanup for this job by myself.

Earlier in my marriage I had wanted to learn to use a chain saw, but my ex had put his foot down on that. He had said that the saw kicks and it would be too dangerous for me.

Now I am single and only use those tree pruners that cut up to an inch thick, which usually gets me by. Yep, I'll have to find someone to clean this up for me.

Wondering about the wound in the tree where the branch snapped from, I looked up. Maybe there was enough of the branch left that it could be sawed off cleanly from the trunk to accelerate the healing process. I had a hard time looking up because the sun was almost at high noon, shining directly in my eyes. My neck was getting a cramp in it from the strain, so I kept moving around the tree to see where the branch fell from. I couldn't see it! Maybe the area was too high for me to see. I continued to look, but saw nothing.

I was about to run into the house to get my sunglasses when a thought crossed my mind. What if there wasn't a wound? Didn't Quem say something about the tree's service? The pieces were slowly coming together when I saw a place on the tree high up that looked like where a branch should be, but wasn't. I was really confounded, but was growing suspicious.

What? I stood there for several minutes, looking all over the tree to make sure I had the right spot. I was sure of it. The wound was gone. Forgetting all about the neighbors, I hollered, "Nathanal!" This was getting too weird for me.

He calmly responded like there was nothing out of the ordinary happening here. "Nakala, what is it?"

I was still staring at the place where the branch had been ripped from the tree. In an accusing tone, I said, "Nathanal, you know what it is. How did the tree heal itself in one day?"

Not wanting to reveal anything, like an expert, he averted the question by commenting on the beautiful weather. He knew I was agitated, so he added, "I am sure it will be discussed when your father gets here."

Curious, I looked at my watch to find that I still had several hours remaining before I would find out anything, so I began to pick up the smaller branches and make a pile. I noticed how green the grass was and made a mental note that I'd have to get my mower serviced soon. Yep, my life was getting stranger every day.

My back was beginning to ache from bending down so many times, so I decided to take a break by walking to the garage to find a bag to use for the branches. I sure hoped I had some left over from last summer. Before I walked to the garage, I stopped and stood up as straight as I could to stretch my back. Before I knew what was happening, I saw flashes of light and I began to get dizzy. Nathanal was right there telling me, "Nakala, bend down and breathe."

Down I went like Nathanal told me. I waited for a minute or two before I stood back up. I noticed beads of perspiration forming on my brow. I felt sick. All I wanted to do was sit down in the grass, so I did. I had been fine two minutes earlier.

Finally, I began to feel a little better, so I went back to my chore of finding the bag for yard waste. As I approached the garage door, another wave of dizziness hit me. This time, I sank to my knees for relief.

While I waited for the dizziness to pass, I noticed that I had landed next to the back porch. My pants were getting wet, so I moved over to sit on the cement pad and noticed a single purple crocus growing in the tiny crack of the walk. I marveled at the tenacity of this little flower.

My breath deepened, smelling the freshness of the grass and the soil. The grass beckoned me to join it. Without thinking, I slid from the porch back onto the grass—the moisture no longer seemed to matter. I sat there and gently touched the tender young blades of grass as if they were *my* children. From a higher perspective, I watched myself push the blades over ever so gently, amazed at how easily they gave without breaking. How resilient they were!

✳ ✳ ✳

I sensed a presence beside me, then a slight pressure on my right shoulder. It was Nathanal. He understood me and knew my feelings of uncertainty. He knew that having my father here was awesome, yet intimidating for me. Quem was here to teach me, and I knew it was serious business. I felt a release of tension and whispered a thank you to God.

Nathanal suddenly announced that we had a visitor. Because I don't ordinarily see my guides, I am either told that I have a visitor or the visitor will announce himself. Sometimes I can feel who it is.

Not knowing if Nathanal meant someone had pulled up to the front of the house or whether it was another guide who was here, I asked Nathanal who it was. He said Samuel Paul had arrived and wanted to speak to me. (Samuel Paul is one of the Pleiadian ascended masters that I work with.) That meant I had to find the journal that I kept specifically for his messages. That meant I'd have to get up. "Not so sure about me getting up, Nathanal," I whispered.

My hand was down on the earth, ready to push myself up, when I felt a pressure in my chest that caused me to pause. I had to work harder to breathe. My vibration had risen as well. I resigned to the feeling and sank back down again, feeling the earth accept my weight.

There was no doubt then that we did have company, and I recognized the energy to be Samuel Paul's. He is quite powerful, and if he gets close to me, my heart beats as if it is under strain. He has that effect on me.

Samuel Paul didn't move back to ease my discomfort or wait for me to acclimate to his energy. "I have come to speak to you. I'd like you to get my book."

Without hesitating, I said, "Of course, Samuel Paul. Would you please give me a moment? I haven't been feeling well. I'd just like to sit here and breathe for a moment."

"Ah, I see," was all he said.

I knew he would assess my energy if he hadn't already.

"My child, you are to rise and go into the house and get a glass of water for yourself. Just go and get it now."

Of course, I got up with the expectation that I'd get dizzy again. So I just whispered to Nathanal to stand by me as I went into the house. I knew that Samuel Paul was correct. I needed to hydrate my body after working like I did. But I shouldn't have become light-headed like I did.

In the house I sat down with my water, did some deep breathing for a few minutes, and felt much better. I managed to exchange pleasantries with Samuel Paul by asking him how he was doing. As always, his response was, "Very well, thank you.

"Miss, we have limited time today, as you know you have Master Quem coming and you must allow yourself time to tend to your personal needs as well. I ask you to get my book so we may begin."

Getting up, I found that I was a bit unsteady and grabbed the table for support. I blurted out, "What is wrong with me?"

Quick to the point, Samuel Paul said, "Oh, you have a bit of an imbalance there."

I couldn't help but laugh at his wit as I countered, "Oh, very funny. Seriously, though, is there something wrong with me?"

His answer was, "Not in the least. You are fine. You merely have an imbalance." This time I didn't laugh. I was annoyed, which I knew he felt without me saying a word. But of course, being me, I had snapped at him without meaning to.

"Samuel Paul, really, if there is a problem here, I would like to know about it and correct it." I knew I sounded impatient and bossy, like he was supposed to do this *thing* for me. Well, I didn't feel good. That was my excuse, anyhow.

Samuel Paul didn't fall into my negativity. Instead, he stopped and channeled a deep breath through me, reminding me to center myself. I followed his lead and continued to breathe until I released the energy and was able to rise above my negativity. Samuel Paul stood by and waited.

"Now," Samuel Paul said, "We should get started. But first, get yourself an apple. Your blood sugar is low."

It was almost as if a light bulb came on, "Oh! That is why I got dizzy outside."

"Yes, this is the answer to your imbalance. You allowed yourself to become imbalanced. What did you eat and drink this morning? Review this, please."

"Uh…okay. I had, umm…what did I have? Oh, I ate…oh, all I had was a cup of coffee. I didn't eat. I forgot. I guess I was so nervous or excited or whatever because Quem is coming today." I felt my face grow hot like I was once again a child who had been caught with her hand in the cookie jar before dinner.

"Precisely," was all Samuel Paul offered.

With feelings of guilt, I ate my apple in silence, wondering how he knew that I hadn't eaten breakfast. I felt myself regaining balance, and the irritation diminished as well.

As if on cue, Samuel Paul began his teaching just as I finished the last bite of the apple. "I must remind you that your physical body is your vehicle throughout this life stream—this incarnation. You must care for it. God has given over this responsibility to you. The physical body is the Temple of God. If you neglect your duty, the body suffers and will ultimately perish.

"We have work to do here, you and all of creation—God's creation. All are divinely connected as One. My desire is not to reprimand you. However, perhaps that is what you require in order to take this concept— this responsibility—seriously! You are no longer a child. You have acknowledged and committed yourself to the task at hand; this is to learn to let go of judgment of self and others."

Samuel Paul continued on, "With your reaction to my one word, 'Precisely,' you were taken back to your childhood and to fear. This occurred so very easily. I'd like to see it not continue…this reacting to another's comments or opinions."

No one ever indicated to me that the lessons would be easy. They are simply fabulous. These guys are able to make something as simple as my not eating breakfast into a lesson that encompasses so much more. I am a work in progress, and I must give myself room to grow. I knew Samuel Paul was correct. I have never known him to not be.

The apple, well, I knew I should find something more to eat. I really didn't feel like having another *talk* like this anytime soon.

Feeling a little uncomfortable for having to take care of my business while he was here, I hesitated before I decided it would be best to announce to Samuel Paul that I thought it would be wise for me to get something more to eat before we began.

The guides often will give me a motion or symbol in my mind's eye instead of talking. This time Samuel Paul chose to use this way of communicating.

To me it looks like someone drawing on an invisible chalkboard with an invisible piece of chalk. There is no one doing the drawing. But I clearly see the motion. Many times I have asked how they draw like that in my mind. The answer is always the same—energy.

The first thing I found to eat was some trail mix. As I poured the contents into a bowl, I decided it was time to really take stock of what I had here. Raisins, almonds, peanuts, sunflower seeds, banana chips, yogurt covered raisins, mango chips, mango flavored pineapple, cranberries, and cashews. Okay, so not all as it appeared. I decided the sugared banana and mango chips perhaps weren't so great.

Gluten has been taken off of my diet, so having a quick slice of toast with jam wasn't an option, although having a crunchy piece of toast was what I truly wanted. Oh, I know there are gluten-free breads, but I just have not ventured that far into this new way of eating.

Samuel Paul read my thoughts and said, "Nakala, why do you choose to deny yourself? You are free to get creative here. Make yourself some gluten-free pancakes, with blueberries and honey. That would certainly satisfy the craving."

My reasoning for not obliging myself was I didn't want to take the time, *his time*. The way I saw it, Samuel Paul's time was far too valuable for me to use on my own trivial needs or wants.

I felt guilty, and consequently I began to make excuses. "Samuel Paul, it takes too long to make pancakes. You have, I am sure, other things to do that are much more important than waiting on me to make pancakes!" I felt ashamed, but what came out was anger. *Oh, God*, I prayed, *what am I doing here, talking to an ascended master like this?*

"Nakala," Samuel Paul began in a reassuring tone, "honey, I have come for you. This is our time. I just explained to you that your body is the Temple of God and it is *your* responsibility to take care of it. I would never expect you to deny your body on my account, not ever! You are to take care of yourself, *always!*"

To my dismay, I heard Samuel Paul direct me, "Now, you make yourself those pancakes, and add some blueberries to the batter as well. I know you enjoy those. In your cabinet there, you have some local honey that you can drizzle on the top to satisfy your palate."

Samuel Paul interjected one other thing before he stood back. "Nakala, remember, this life is a gift from God. Enjoy all that you do."

That was Samuel Paul's way of telling me to be conscious of my thoughts and emotions—to go into gratitude as I prepared and ate my meal. This would raise the vibration of my food and myself, allowing it (the body) to accept and digest the food more easily.

The pancakes were delicious and I did enjoy them. I thanked Samuel Paul for his encouragement and assured him that I would take better care of my body from then on.

I figured it was time for *the* talk from Samuel Paul. So I went to find his book and sat down in my chair. I waited for a couple of minutes and nothing happened. No one spoke. I wondered if he were still here. It isn't like I can see him. He could have easily slipped out without saying a word to me. The feeling of disappointment to the point of rejection and abandonment started to creep in.

Suddenly, without any outer prompting, I began to pray. *My Father in heaven, the Highest Most Creative Awareness, please join me and work through me for the highest good of all of creation.*

Setting my intention on love and gratitude, I felt my vibration rise, and all of the tension that I had created from not hearing Samuel Paul's reassuring voice quickly disappeared.

Sometimes the guides just disappear without ever saying a thing. Kind of strange that they do that, I thought.

Then, without any prior hint, I heard Samuel Paul ask if I were ready to receive.

Taking a deep breath, I answered, "Yes, I am ready to receive." I gave him my full attention and opened his book, found his last transmission, and got my pencil ready.

"What I have for you today may come as a bit of a surprise or maybe a bit more like a revelation of sorts. Your father, Quem, has told me that he intends to stay in your area for some time.

"Quem and Sarah are stationed nearby and desire to work with you while they are here."

The thoughts and feelings came all jumbled up. I was surprised and grateful! Although, my feelings might have been equivalent to having a bombshell dropped in my lap to have Quem and Sarah work with me. I always wanted to have Quem return as my primary teacher, but since we finished *When Angels Speak: Book One, The Awakening a Pleiadian Endeavor,* Quem had delegated my care out, putting Babaró (Bar-Bare-o), who is another guide, in charge. Did this mean that Quem and Sarah were back for good, or just a short stay?

My mind was open for any information Samuel Paul was willing to give me concerning Sarah and Quem. The idea of Sarah being here intrigued me as well, as she has stated plainly that my father would be teaching me. She would stand back. And stand back she has. I can count on one hand the times Sarah has come to speak to me. Each was a major event and such a special gift.

When Sarah speaks to me I definitely feel that motherly love and guidance, but her mannerism is also regal, as if she comes from royalty: She does not mince words. I really want to get to know her better. Maybe during this stay we will have the opportunity to become closer.

Sarah seems to want to wait to work with me. Perhaps she will never work with me like Quem has. I don't know. But I feel that Sarah has remained more aloof or distant. Her explanation to me was that there is plenty of time for us to reacquaint ourselves with one another.

Samuel Paul was waiting for me and brought me back from my thoughts when he calmly began to speak to me again. "Nakala, your mother and father intend to take this time to work with you on the upcoming book."

My heart skipped a beat. I managed to utter only one word, "Wow." I took a couple of seconds to center myself, then asked, "The upcoming book? What do you mean? I am working on the second volume of *When Angels Speak,* with Babaró. What do you mean?"

Again, my thoughts wandered off. I was well on my way with the second book and they were going to take me off of it? All I could think of was all of the work—the months of work I had put into this project. Well, I was certainly confused by this new plan.

For some reason, I just stopped trying to figure out what was going on. Time and time again I thought I had known their reasoning or understood their plan, but was shown later that I had not a single clue what their real intentions were. I have learned the hard way that it simply isn't worth the effort to even think on this. I waited for Samuel Paul to give me the full explanation. No more asking questions here—I was finished.

Samuel Paul began, "As you know, with the New Year many shifts have taken place. All higher realms of intelligence reassess positions of leadership during particular cycles. The different councils of light are no different. Those leadership positions trickle down into the different spheres. When I speak of spheres, I am referring to different levels of ability, desire, and so on to lead within planetary and star systems and even tribes such as ours—the Akasie.

"Just as the New Year rolled around, some masters that you were not accustomed to communicating with visited you. You were informed that they were at your home on business to make the necessary assessments concerning the work you do as a channel and a writer. These masters were looking at all levels as to your abilities and focus—even your level of desire concerning the service you are involved in. In essence, they were looking at your area of expertise of service and how well you perform it! They want to know where each student is at and the progress that has been made since the last assessment. Your health was even considered. Every level of your being was measured and considered for the work that you are doing and are planning to do.

"You were given the words that *all* projects were to go on hold until all had been reviewed. Your book was part of the collection that was to be put on hold. I tell you, even how you accepted this news was taken into consideration.

"New leadership was at hand, and with any new leadership, new ideas come forth. They would be making decisions on whether or not to proceed on certain evolutionary projects.

"In addition, each project they felt a worthwhile endeavor to proceed with would be assessed for appropriate changes to improve the quality of its purpose.

"It was then that you understood that always there are fluctuations in the energy. Because of these fluctuations, adjustments are made accordingly. This is in direct correlation to certain projects (even finished ones, published or not) that may be laid down temporarily or even permanently. New ideas to meet the criteria of educating the masses are considered. All must be in alignment to continue.

"So you see, Quem, as your father and master, was very much a part of this process. During this time, Careese, one of your guides. took another position—a higher position with more authority and responsibility.

"To sum this up, many changes took place during this time, including the direction of your work, and subsequently your life."

At this point, Samuel Paul had my attention. The words "your life" held a certain ambiguity. "Samuel Paul, exactly what are you getting at? Is some major change regarding my relationships or where I live or possibly even my work about to change?" I was reserved, yet apprehensive as to where this conversation was going.

To my thorough astonishment, Samuel Paul closed the conversation by saying, "Nakala, the time grows nigh for your father's arrival. You have your own personal needs to attend to. I must take leave. The books will continue on. Know this, as it is your life's purpose and what brings you much pleasure."

I felt the beautiful love from Samuel Paul just before he said goodbye.

CHAPTER
FIVE

It was 2 p.m. The time had flown by. I had to get some lunch and rest. I also wanted to meditate before Quem got here. I felt it would be beneficial to sit and reflect on what Samuel Paul had shared with me, but unfortunately, all of that would have to wait.

I wondered if Quem would appear like he had yesterday in a cloud of vapor or would he communicate with me like Samuel Paul had, donning his cloak of invisibility? One never knows about those with powers beyond a human's scope of understanding. I wanted to not second-guess them anymore. It simply took too much of my energy. I was determined to not allow my curiosity to get in the way again.

The time drew near for Quem's arrival, and I began to feel a little apprehensive. Recognizing that my body was becoming tense, I deliberately shifted my thoughts and began to look at the meeting with Quem like I was preparing to have a client come for a channeled reading. Then I shifted how I felt even more by thinking of what a blessing it is to receive such a gift!

I wanted to make a pot of tea, find my journal, and get a pencil before Quem arrived. Having a few extra moments allowed me to look over yesterday's entries and select some specific material that I wanted clarification on. I guess I became rather absorbed in what I was doing, because I forgot to watch for clouds of energy. Instead, I heard Quem's voice and looked up and saw him standing in the doorway, looking refreshed. His face had a radiant, even jovial, appearance to it, as if he had been out for a run.

Automatically, I placed my hands together as if going into prayer and bent my body forward in a gesture of respect to welcome him.

Quem began by telling me, "Nakala, it would do you well to get yourself a bouquet of flowers to grace your presence."

I hesitated before speaking. "I do love flowers, but...flowers, umm; I have a torn opinion concerning that. Wouldn't cutting flowers shorten their life? Wouldn't cutting the flowers hurt them? They do have feelings."

"Miss," he began, "Flowers are much like the trees here. They are here to serve. Flowers serve by giving forth beauty and stimulating all of your senses. The beauty of a flower can bring a person into a state of bliss. Know this, my daughter; their gift is their desire to give unto you."

Quem really didn't answer my question, so I asked again. "Yes, but doesn't the cut hurt them?"

In response Quem offered, "Give thanks for this gift. Do not take for granted the beauty that it graces you with. Include these beings in your prayers, thanking them for their service. This is what you are to do with all life forms and intelligences. When you offer this energy of gratitude, they receive and are pleased to give over their energy to you." He paused for a moment as if in contemplation, then added, "Perhaps to have a flowering potted plant would be more pleasing to you?"

Quem didn't wait for my answer; he continued, "The maple tree out there suffered for the purpose of gifting you with the lesson you received. Because of his gift, the masters gave back by healing the wound. Your guides gathered around this being last night and gave forth great streams of light to assist the tree in sealing the wound, thus preventing it from further stress. We were happy to assist in this manner."

Being overcome by his words, tears began to fall down my cheeks, dripping on the pages of my journal. I hadn't realized that the masters would expend their energy for a tree. I was so grateful for this act of kindness that I was almost at a loss for words. "Quem, what can I do to repay you for what you have done for me? You have healed my tree, and for that I am grateful."

Quem cleared his throat before he started his teaching. "First, my young daughter, be it known that I would be honored if you would acknowledge me as your father by addressing me with the title Father in all communications. This would please me beyond measure."

Ah, I had sensed this, but I felt like it wasn't my place to change the way I addressed him. I had called him Father yesterday without consciously intending to.

I stopped in mid-sentence and looked up into my father's clear blue eyes. There was a softness to his eyes, almost a vulnerability there. I saw the tears begin to well up in them. My breath caught in my throat and I couldn't speak for a moment. "Of course I will address you as Father."

I felt torn with the idea of calling Quem Father, but I felt it respectful to do so. I already had a father, so I asked, "Should I call you Father or Father Quem?"

Quem was still listening to my thoughts. I watched his face, waiting for some clue as to how he felt. He didn't speak for a moment, as if he was thinking about it. Then he said, "I'd like it if you would address me as Father Quem and your mother as Mother Sarah. I understand this is not how you are accustomed to addressing your elders, but as it is, that is how my children speak to me and of me. You still have your parents on this Earth, and for ease of identification, what I ask of you will work quite well."

I wanted to respond with something profound, but instead all I could think of to say was, "Yes, I will be honored to do as you ask."

Again, I had wandered off with my thoughts, and Quem stood back waiting for me to formulate them. I was weighing the implications of a title like "Father" and what in my world it could signify. Calling him Father Quem felt weird to me. I felt almost self-conscious to use that title. I took it as a formal title of higher authority. The title almost had a religious connotation to it. I asked, "Don't some religious sects call their priests Father? I'd have to do some research, but aren't the nuns called Mother in the Catholic religion?" I couldn't help asking, "Are you a priest of some sort?"

There was a reverence to his demeanor, and his voice softened with his reply. "I am a high master and teacher. The Akasie family must have those who are willing to teach the universal laws to those who are masters in their own right. I work with my family, the Akasie, to teach them the steps to spiritual mastery.

"There are many other teachers who have their doctorates in areas such as music, the arts, or perhaps astronomy or physics."

I was beginning to see that perhaps I was not really his daughter in the literal sense, but someone that he had taken on to oversee as I made my way through the dense energies of the third dimension.

Quickly Father Quem addressed my thoughts by saying, "You are correct that I oversee those who have ventured here and require guidance. I spend time overseeing those here in this plane as well as at Myra, Pleiades. In addition, I travel extensively as I serve on the Council of Light, as I am an ambassador of the Galactic Federation.

"However, you are incorrect in your assumption. I am your father in the literal sense. Your origins begin in the Pleiades. Your mother, Sarah, and I gave birth to your energy. This concept you do not recognize, nor do you understand. At some point I will talk to you in length about this so you may understand in fullness your beginning.

"For now, know that I am your master teacher and your father. I love you and desire to be of assistance in your ascension, going from the third dimension to the fifth dimension. It would give me great pleasure and joy to serve you in this way."

I felt as if something had shifted—as if this was my choice to have him work with me. "What? Are you asking for *my* permission to serve me?" Father Quem stopped cold in his tracks, his expression serious as he stated boldly, "You know, Nakala, you must ask for assistance on this path. Without it I can do nothing."

I really wasn't quite sure what was happening here. I had already asked for his guidance and do ask every single day. *Why was he talking like this?*

I stopped writing and looked up again into Father Quem's eyes. This time I looked deeply into his eyes and I saw him and felt the purity of his soul. I felt his love overtake my senses and open my heart. In that moment, I felt I could not possibly describe in words of any sort on a piece of paper or even with my voice the true and profound effect this exchange had on me. His love was so pure that I simply surrendered to it and joined with him in the exchange of love. I felt a peace flow through me, and I understood his truth, his desire, and his wisdom!

After a few moments, Father Quem calmly said, "Let's just say, we are reaffirming our vows to be true to one another and committed for the highest good to serve all of creation.

"With that said, I bring it to you that you will be traveling to Sedona, Arizona in three weeks' time." I was stunned by the information and how easily Father Quem had delivered it. Father Quem had given me this information like it was no big deal. Then he added, "Samuel Paul will be gifting you with our next book in *The Accounts of a Pleiadian Traverler* series, entitled *In the Light of Day,* but beforehand, I understand you have a trip scheduled to Kansas City."

My mind went into fast mode and the questions began to present themselves. Arizona? How far is that? How long is the drive? Where will I stay? How long will I be staying? The questions continued. In order to quiet myself, I got up to get the world atlas and flipped to the Arizona page. I had never been to Arizona.

The news that I would be traveling to Sedona threw me into a tailspin. There were so many things that I thought I should know. I felt my heart quicken and with it my voice took on a tone that I didn't recognize. I felt excited, yet really if I were honest I'd have to say, quite frankly, I was scared. To cover up my fear, I began to put my energy into my questions about where I'd stay and how long I'd be there. His response was, "The details are being seen to by your Nathanal. You will be receiving the information shortly."

This type of directive had happened before, but this time was a little different. I had just moved back to my hometown to be near both of my aging parents. My father had just been moved into a nursing home a short while ago and was still adjusting. My mother, along with a friend of hers, was now preparing to move in with me so I could watch over them a little closer. Both of my parents are in their late eighties. I wondered what the wisdom in leaving the area so soon could be. In my opinion, there wasn't any!

However, I didn't outwardly express my concern. This year alone, my travels had been quite extensive and all resulted from the direction of my guides. I have learned to follow and have faith that all is in order and for the highest good.

Father Quem sat patiently until I gained control of my mind. Once my thoughts were quiet he began to speak again. "You have a meeting in Kansas City that you have been planning to attend for several weeks now. We desire that you keep that commitment and attend. You have some other errands to do while you are there. Tend to it all. See your friends and your daughter as well."

He ended his instructions by telling me that Nathanal would fill me in with the details when all was in alignment to do so.

Father Quem paused long enough for me to begin to think perhaps our meeting was complete before he began to speak again. "Nakala, there are a few other areas of interest that I'd like to bring forth just now. I am well aware of who you keep company with." I took his tone to be of some sort of reprimand, but I couldn't be sure. *Did he put emphasis on the word who?*

All of a sudden I felt like I was been scrutinized somehow…judged. I really didn't like the implications of it all. *What exactly did he mean by that?* I felt like a child again and my face flushed from embarrassment … guilt.

One of my errands to Kansas City would be to pick up some of my clothing from my friend Allen's house. Well, I guess now he is an ex-friend. I had tried to make it work, but many times I found myself impatient and angry when I was with him. *Could this be who Father Quem was referring to?* God, I hoped not, because this could get really ugly.

The really crazy part of this so-called "friendship," or lack thereof, was that our guides were playing Cupid with us, and for the life of me, I was unable to understand why they had picked this man! Although, I had to admit that I did recognize that Allen was nice enough and certainly had some of the qualities I was looking for in a man.

Father Quem looked at me questioningly, his eyebrows arched. Yet, he had that all-knowing look. Oh, he knew, all right. I began to breathe deeply, silently praying that he would *not go there.*

I tried to console myself by looking at the other side of this. Just what did Father Quem know? Oh, right, everything. He said he was always connected to me and in charge of my lessons, but really, how connected is he? How many of the details did he know? Above all, I did not want to get into this conversation. This is private stuff!

Quem pointedly rattled off several questions to me. "Nakala, honestly, who do you think I am? What do you think my intentions are? Do you understand my abilities? Nakala, do you think I would place you with a man (and I did, know it) if the joining were not for the highest good?"

I didn't answer Father Quem because I hadn't gotten on board with this highest good thing that they are always talking about. From the very beginning the whole relationship with Allen had baffled me. The highest good could simply mean that I was being tested for my ability to discern what *was* for my highest good—in other words, I was going through a lesson.

Father Quem had taught me early on that I was to follow my heart. "Do what makes your heart sing," was what he had told me on countless occasions. I knew there was a connection with Allen; I just hadn't figured out on what level I was supposed to be connected with him.

For thirty-five years I was married, but no more. I had chosen to go my way. After that many years, to date someone is quite unfamiliar. I know the qualities I want in a man, but I don't know what is for my highest good. Maybe I should not even be involved with anyone, at least not now, when I feel conflicted.

I still hadn't answered Father Quem's question. Instead, I side-stepped him a little to delay the embarrassment that I figured was inevitable and then I asked him, "Do you want me to answer your questions?" I really wasn't sure at this point what he wanted, but I knew what *I* wanted: a way out.

CHAPTER
SIX

From the very beginning, I had known that meeting Allen was no coincidence. One evening, out of the blue, he had come to one of my channeled group readings. That night we were working with Archangel Jeremiel.

After the channeling was over, we all had a snack and spent some time talking to get to know one another. I decided to ask Allen some questions. Allen hadn't been on the RSVP list. I began by asking him how he had heard about the channeling, what type of work he did, and what not. Then I asked him how he ended up coming to the channeling. Allen didn't shift the question or even stop to think about it. He said with clarity and conviction that when he saw the flyer he *knew* that he was to be at the reading. Without any prompting, he added that he rarely went to *these things*.

* * *

Father Quem brought me back from my reverie by telling me, "Yes, I'd like you to answer my questions. Would you like me to repeat them for you? You seem to be a little distracted here."

My breath caught and I felt like I just wanted to run and hide. Unfortunately, there would be none of that. So I sucked in another long, slow breath and said, "No, Father Quem, I can answer your questions without you repeating them to me."

Instead, of answering his questions right away, though, I began to breathe deeply to bring myself back to center. Somehow, I felt I was using the breathing as an avoidance tactic, but I knew I had to get my head on straight, and quickly. My emotions were raw concerning Allen. I knew Quem would eventually get to how I felt as well.

My head cleared somewhat and I proceeded. "Okay, I am going to start by saying that I know that you are my father and I know without a shadow of a doubt that you are here to teach me; these lessons are for my highest good. I know you love me and want what is best for me. How well you actually watch over me, I do not know. I do know that you have told me that I can contact you anytime if I need you."

Pushing aside the anxiety I felt, my strength began to build and I allowed myself to speak up and say my truth. "As for getting Allen to come to the channeling that night, I have no idea what that was *really* about. You say it was for my highest good to meet and work with him.

"As far as I know, it could have been for my highest good to have acknowledged what I was feeling in my gut, which was an aversion to his manner." I stopped speaking, and thought of that night; I remembered it well. Allen had lingered at the house long after everyone else had gone. I was still high from doing the channeling and knew it would be some time before I would sleep.

I felt divided that night with Allen. Part of me wanted to send him on his way, directly after the group had gone. There was something there I felt that was akin to fear. I think I allowed him to stay longer because my ego was doing the waltz. Allen had shown an interest in me as a person—a woman, not just someone who has the ability to channel archangels and other beings of light.

So instead of sending him on his way, I allowed him to stay for quite some time after everyone else had left. What Allen said about being guided to the channeling, "I just knew I was to be here," had intrigued me somewhat. I thought maybe there was more to the story, so I just went with it.

"So you see, Father, I do not really know your intentions concerning this particular teaching."

My emotions had opened up…running deep. I was filled with an elusive, dark substance. It seemed my emotions were all slippery. I couldn't get a good grip on them to understand how I felt.

Stopping my speech, I gathered my thoughts to assess if I wanted to continue on or not. Suddenly, I realized full force that I had to face this thing. I knew that Father Quem was well aware of the situation concerning Allen and myself, but I was the one who had to lay it out on the table, nonetheless.

"Father," I continued, "Allen and I have decided to not see each other again. The problem is, I accidentally left behind some of my clothes at his house. If what I had left was something I didn't care about, I would not bother going back to pick them up. I do not want to see him again." As I said the words I could feel my heart. There was a definite ache there. The feelings I had were totally preposterous. I could hear myself ranting, "My mind says run. My heart says…I don't know. How stupid is this? We do not get along." For some reason, I thought I had to justify my feelings and actions to Father Quem.

"Nakala," he began, "I would like you to stop and listen to my words carefully now. I am your father and your master. My intentions are honorable, as I *only* want what is best for you.

"My abilities far exceed your understanding at all levels. I watch over you closely, always. I know what and who you are involved with and how you are thinking and feeling, *always!* In addition, I see and feel your actions.

"This man, Allen, was brought into your life for many reasons. He agreed with us—and you, I will add, agreed as well—to assist in teaching each other a few things. This was done on a higher level of awareness. Your lower self is not privy to this information, as of yet."

He paused to allow me to express myself if I wanted to. I did!

"Father Quem," I said, "Look, I remember one of the first teachings you gave me was to follow my heart. But this time I am not so sure. I like Allen…a lot, but when I am with him I become unbalanced. For one thing, when I am with him I don't get enough rest. His rhythms are almost opposite to mine. On three specific occasions, and I remember them exceedingly well, I have left his home with the intention of never returning. Then somehow, for some trivial reason, we end up calling one another, and the whole thing begins again. I feel like I am on an emotional rollercoaster with steep grades. I never liked roller coaster rides, and I want off."

With a surge of anger, I threw down my pencil. I felt out of control and was too upset to continue. My tears gathered strength and threatened to spill over. I bowed my head, working to hide my vulnerability, as if somehow it were a bad thing. I could not contain my emotion any longer and felt the hot tear-drops roll down my cheeks and gather on my chin. Then I heard a tiny plop on the page of my journal, drawing my attention to how utterly stupid this must look—how stupid I felt. My embarrassment grew.

I wanted out of there, and fast. My mind raced to find a reason to leave. *Tissue, I need a tissue* was all I could think. I didn't want to look Father Quem in the eye, so I got up as I muttered a lame excuse and headed for the bathroom. I shut the door harder than I intended to and grabbed a tissue. Then I grabbed another one. I blew my nose, waited a moment, hoping the tears would subside, and blew again.

How come I was acting this way? I certainly didn't want to. I was embarrassed and ashamed. To put off going back in the living room, I freshened up a bit. Then I got a glass of water and drank it slowly. That always helps. When I was finished, I knew it was time to face up to whatever this was.

Then the thought crossed my mind that it was entirely possible that Father Quem might have decided that I (or better yet he) had had enough and made a quiet exit.

My journey back into my living room—back into the same room where Quem sat waiting for me—made me feel like a small child when I had walked into a classroom full of people. I was the center of attention—every eye trained on me. I felt vulnerable—judged—like I didn't measure up in some area. They could see my flaws—my secrets—and certainly could see that I was uncomfortable. I'd just as soon jump out the window than talk about Allen to my Father, Quem.

Well, Father Quem was still there. He sat there on the couch, just like I had left him. The only difference was that he had taken my journal and was leafing through the pages, picking out certain passages and reading them. What he was looking for, I had no idea.

This is different, I thought, as I sat back down as quietly as possible. He seemed immersed in his task, so I decided not to interrupt his perusal.

Father Quem stopped long enough to look up and acknowledge my presence with a nod. He did not smile or display any emotion. From his manner, one might assume that he had forgotten my colorful display of emotion a few minutes ago and was purely absorbed in what he was reading. He lifted the book in my direction as he asked, "Do you mind?"

Trying not to interrupt him, I quietly said, "Not at all, take as long as you like."

Several excruciating minutes passed while I sat and watched Father Quem flip through page after page, stopping every now and again to read certain passages. He slowly shut the book, looked at me, and smiled. "Nakala, I am pleased with your work—your documentation. However," he paused for a dramatic effect, "I'd like you to expand your work to include some identification of your emotions throughout your writing."

He continued, "After you have identified your feelings, it would benefit you greatly to look at each situation and see what specific event has triggered each and every emotion."

What surprised me was when he looked at me and said, "Honey, I am not only referring to what triggers negative emotions but what stirs the positive emotions—the heart—as well. Find out what brings about the feelings of love, compassion, and gratitude. Learn to recognize when these feelings emerge, and please focus on the positive. We will build on this as we go forward."

Before Father Quem gave me this assignment, I had felt utterly defeated, and questioned the sense of going on. Now, just a few minutes later, with a simple observation and some encouraging words I felt like I could pick up where I left off and continue to go forward.

Father Quem was ready to address some of my concerns. "Now, Nakala, I know that you feel that you are against the wall, so to speak. You have been directed to work with Allen. There is no error in this guidance, my guidance. Unfortunately, you have allowed yourself to gravitate toward the negative concerning Allen. You are assessing every discipline and habit he has because you feel we have placed you together to be as a couple. You are not in error. For your highest good, you are to be joined as a couple."

In defiance, I vigorously shook my head no, not wanting to hear what he had to say. Father Quem didn't acknowledge my not so subtle communication.

"I believe the assignment I gave you earlier concerning your emotions will assist you greatly with this union."

I had to stop Father Quem. I was in disbelief that he would want me to continue the relationship with Allen. *That is what he was saying, right?* The words that he had spoken played back in my head. He wanted me to have a relationship with this guy. The same man who pushed every last button I had? *This couldn't be correct. I must have misunderstood something here.*

I asked myself, "What is the use in formulating questions with this man? He hears everything I think even before I say it. *I have free will here, right?*" I realized I had begun to argue with myself. *What is the use of having free will if I can't use it?*

Quite unexpectedly, Father Quem stood up as if to take his leave, but instead he walked to the window to look out and began talking about the work I had done on the yard.

Oh, he was good, alright. He was using a strategic move here. I saw it clearly.

Just then he turned to face me with a smile and chuckled almost to himself, but loud enough that I heard him. He had this way of easing my anxiety.

All of a sudden, I just said, "I love you. You do know that, right?"

"Of course I know this, Nakala. You are my daughter, and no matter what our course, the love shall remain between us and grow ever stronger over the days to come.

"Your friend, Allen, is a strong, compassionate fellow. I did not just pick him up off the street. He is of the Akasie family, just as you are. He is in the same soul family. Allen works with you in some respect each time you incarnate.

"We sat in council—all of us, your guides and yourselves—before the two of you incarnated this go-around. We set before you a direction on your path and the roles you would play to assist one another in the process of your ascension to the fifth dimension. Your meeting Allen was meant to occur and meant to occur precisely at the time it occurred.

"Understand that Allen has an entirely different background as you."

I heard myself grumble and say out loud, "I think that may be the understatement of the year."

Father Quem continued on, as if I had not said a word. "Yes, he has chosen parents that had an entirely different lifestyle than your parents. This was done for purpose. The blending of the two of you is extreme in nature but perfect, as it will enable you to finish your life lessons, taking you into the higher realms of ascension."

None of what he was saying was being recorded. My focus was no longer on writing. Somewhere during his message, I had laid down my pencil, wondering what was going to happen to me. I watched in fascination as he spoke about my life like it was all mapped out and I had absolutely no say concerning it.

Suddenly, to my astonishment, I began to laugh hysterically. I couldn't stop, but at the same time I was quite aware of what I was doing and knew it was inappropriate—how I looked. I felt rather silly. I couldn't get along with this guy, Allen, and Father Quem was talking like the two of us, as a couple, was a done deal! *Oh, God, I need a rest.*

Allen and I had barely spoken to each other since that fateful day three weeks ago—the last time I said I had had enough and walked out. I did call him two days ago to give him an idea of when I would come to retrieve my things from his house. That in itself had been rather awkward. On the inside I felt shy, but I managed to present myself in a dignified and business-like manner. I hadn't been able to read Allen's energy, as he spoke in a very detached manner with no emotion. *Was he angry with me? Did he hate me? Did he know that the guides had this plan and were telling me we were supposed to be together?*

Allen trusts his intuition as I do and clearly understands that we have guides, masters, and angels who are guiding us the best they can. However, up until now he has not been aware of any other way to communicate with his guides other than to have someone channel his messages. In other words, he has been unable to hear his guides speak to him.

My guides asked me specifically to teach Allen to use a pendulum so he would be able to at least ask yes or no questions. I shared the directive that I was given with Allen. In addition, I shared my feelings of why using a device like this might not be such a great idea. The conclusion of our conversation had been that I disapproved of the use of this device, as it had proven to be extremely limiting for in-depth communication purposes. His stance on the subject was unshakable. He was determined to learn how to use the pendulum. But no matter what my opinion was on the subject, when I asked my guides (and I asked them several times, thinking that there had to be a mistake) if it would be for the highest good to teach him, they told me in a very strong voice, "Yes!"

So I had done what I was told and had gone ahead and taught him how to use the pendulum to the very best of my ability.

I am well aware that Allen's guides are having him use the pendulum as a step. Of course they want to communicate with him. I get it! But I have had firsthand experience with this device, and I have seen how easy it is to formulate questions that are open-ended without realizing what is happening.

In other words, questions must be asked to receive a yes or no answer. If you are counting on the answer to assist you in a life-altering event and get the wrong answer…well, you get my drift.

In addition, you may ask a question that is too vague or that the guides choose not to answer. In both cases the answer that you will receive will be a no. The person may take it literally, thinking that the answer to the question is simply a no.

Back when I had been teaching Allen to use the pendulum, Nathanal told me, "Nakala, let go of your fear concerning Allen's new skill. It is a gift. He is learning. Go into celebration concerning Allen's acceptance of this new way of communication with his guides, his newfound ability. Look at it as if he is taking a class. We will call it *Learning to Communicate with Your Spirit Guides 101!*"

Allen is superior when it comes to meditating. He is totally dedicated to his practice. At first, I was totally impressed by it all. But then I saw how many hours he meditated, and I felt threatened by it. Why? I am not entirely sure.

Suddenly, Father Quem interrupted my thought process by saying, "Let's direct this conversation to a particular event. You are the one who is insecure in your friendship with Allen, as you have called it. We all know it is more than insecurity that you are feeling, much more. Allen knows deep in his heart what this, the two of you, is about."

Again, I began to shake my head no. I couldn't make sense of this at all. I didn't want to be with Allen. He was too different. Why, he was almost an exact opposite of me in the way he performed in his daily life. He was simply not the kind of man I was looking for.

Father Quem was not taking no for an answer. "Nakala, did you not hear a word I said? Do you not remember our vow to work together for the highest good? If we are going to work together, you are to at least show me some respect by listening to what I have to say before exercising that free will that you cherish so much. I remind you that you have given forth a decree to God Himself that you surrendered to His Will. Perhaps you should revisit that statement and your commitment."

Oh, Father Quem had me, alright. I had been working to allow this guidance for the highest good. I had seen, firsthand, the unlimited power of the Divine. It was my ego that kept stepping in and messing things up.

"Father Quem," I began, "I apologize for my behavior. I know there are some major things that are bothering me, and I haven't allowed myself to let go and be. Can you please forgive me?"

I felt Father Quem's love pour through my body. That was my answer.

"I have a surprise for you, my daughter." Father Quem's disclosure took me off guard. "Your trip to Kansas City will prove to be a busy occasion. You are to see Allen as if it is a new beginning. Allow yourself to relax with him. Allow yourself to really *see* him—his essence."

Did I hear Father Quem's words correctly? I figured that after what I had done, Allen would feel that I am one of *those* women who are high maintenance—and a definite lost cause. Perhaps it would be better for Allen to go on without me.

"You, Nakala, have my directive for now. It is time for us to tend to other tasks at hand. Your mother and I will be watching over you. Know this. We will come for you again."

We said our goodbyes and exchanged the love energy before he walked into the next room, as if to retrieve something. Wow. He had such a commanding presence and his teachings were so focused. I decided to just let my feelings concerning Allen drop. When I saw Allen again I would know what to do…I hoped.

CHAPTER
SEVEN

My trip to Kansas City was the following weekend, and I had plenty of things to do to prepare for it. The first thing I did was talk with my mother to let her know that I was going to Kansas City for a long weekend.

My mother is well aware that I work with my guides and that when I travel I follow Spirit. So I just go where and when I am directed. But nevertheless, my mother asked when I'd be returning. I said that I thought I'd be home Monday but couldn't be sure. Her response was, "I know."

My mother seemed okay with that news, so I decided to go ahead and let her know about the Sedona trip. Being concerned about her feelings and her physical welfare, I carefully watched her body language as I told her the news. She shifted her weight, paused, and then in a small voice that betrayed her insecurity asked how long I'd be gone.

I went ahead and repeated what Father Quem had told me, which was precious little. "Mom," I began, "I am not sure of the dates. You know I'll call you to check in with you." Then I added, "I'll let you know as soon as I know the details."

Up until that point I hadn't thought about how much time I had before I needed to have my little Honda packed and be on the road. I had only the rest of that day and the next to get ready to leave for Kansas City.

As the day progressed, Nathanal gave me bits and pieces of what I was to accomplish while I was in Kansas City. I began making calls to the people that I wanted to connect with while I was there. Everything fell into place, like God Himself had orchestrated the entire thing. I was amazed and grateful that everything was working out so well.

While in the midst of preparing for my trip, Nathanal informed me to plan to be gone to Arizona for approximately four to six weeks. I was stunned. I shook my head in disbelief before I asked, "Why so long?" That is a long time to be away from home. I was looking at the fact that I'd have to drive myself and secure living arrangements ahead of time. Then the cost of the trip came to the forefront of my mind and I began to stew over it. I wondered how I would pull this one off.

Nathanal continued to talk to me about the trip and said that I would be working on the next book while I was away. I would be in seclusion and would not be bothered by anyone. This meant that the phone conversations would be kept to a minimum. (There would be a few people I'd have to let know about my plans.) I asked how I would be able to complete a book in that length of time. Nathanal simply stated that Samuel Paul would discuss that with me.

At one point, I got the atlas out of my car to look at the map of Arizona. Then I looked at the United States map and the highways. I wanted to get an idea of my route and what cities I would be driving through. I found Sedona and what was around that area.

Finally, I asked Nathanal if I should be making reservations for someplace to stay. He gave me an emphatic, "No, all is to come into alignment." I understood what he meant, but that didn't stop me from feeling like there wasn't a safety net under me.

This was huge for me. This idea to send me nearly halfway across the United States, with no one along to physically support me and no clear-cut plans on where I was to stay, would certainly test my faith on every level.

Tuesday night, Nathanal decided for whatever reason to let me know more of his plan and said, "Nakala, get your map out. Find Arizona."

I did as directed. At first I didn't know what I was looking for, so I looked at the area around Sedona, noticing for the first time that there were a lot of mountain ranges in the area.

Nathanal began to speak about the trip. "Nakala, we will be staying in Prescott."

Just when I asked, "Where is Prescott, anyway?" I saw the dot for the city located a little to the southwest of Sedona. Nathanal said, "We will go to Sedona first, then on to Prescott."

Being curious, like I am, I wanted to pump Nathanal for as much information as I could, so I proceeded to ask a couple of questions. "Why are we going to Prescott? What is there?"

Nathanal had his reasons for keeping quiet and refrained from answering. Typical.

* * *

Wednesday morning came early. Kansas City, here I come! I felt an anticipation—a newness. The time was barely 6 a.m. My Honda was packed and I was backing out the driveway, heading for a new adventure. My first stop was the Quick Shop to fill up my gas tank and get a cappuccino.

The entire day had been planned in segments to get as much done as possible. On my way I made a stop in a suburb of Kansas City where I used to live, to take a friend of mine, along with my daughter, for an early lunch at one of our favorite Mexican diners.

After lunch I had an appointment with my old beautician for a haircut and style. (I still hadn't found anyone down in the Wichita area that I liked as well.) I hoped to look my best for when I saw Allen, so getting a 'do would be perfect. Allen was next on my list.

The last time I had spoken to Allen, I told him I thought I'd be at his place Wednesday afternoon sometime. I wasn't sure about the time and would have to call him when I knew more.

When I was finished getting my hair done, I called Allen and told him I'd be there in 10-15 minutes and told him that I'd just like to visit with him for a few minutes if I could. I was nervous about seeing him again. Fear had settled in about how he would treat me. Neither of us addressed our feelings. He just said, "Okay," and we hung up.

The traffic was insane going over to Allen's, which didn't help my anxiety. I recognized that I was extremely anxious about seeing Allen again. I didn't want to feel this way. What I wanted was to be composed and in control of myself. The last thing I wanted to do was *feel*. Focusing on my stomach, I recognized that stress had taken residence, making my body tight. Yes, I had a tad bit of fear going on. Specifically, I was fretting over the mistakes I had made concerning Allen and how he would treat me when I got there.

I reminded myself that I was looking at what had happened in our past. There was nothing I could do to change it. I had apologized to him, and that was as much as I could do.

Worrying about what was in front me was a total waste of energy as well. All I could do was make the best of it. What it came down to was whether Allen would open his door for me or not.

In my mind, I replayed Father Quem's words (that Allen and I were to be joined), only ending up with more anxiety.

There I was, crawling through rush hour traffic on I-435 in construction, talking to myself out loud. I really needed to let go of the anxiety.

Several miles down the highway I saw that the traffic was not getting any better and I became conscious of the fact that people may be looking at me.

Nathanal was sitting beside me but was so quiet that I had completely forgotten he was there until the anxiety had peaked. Without intending to I yelled, "A couple? How can I possibly be his wife when I don't even like him half of the time?" I didn't stop there. I continued to analyze every conceivable angle to foresee every possible outcome. Truly, I did not want any surprises when I got to Allen's.

Nathanal clearly didn't want to get in the middle of this livid conversation with myself, but he did anyway. With a controlled voice, he asked me, "Nakala, what are you thinking? Look at it. Look at where you are at in this very moment." That was enough to pull me back to center.

As I pulled into Allen's driveway, I saw him standing behind the gate, smoking a cigarette. He was waiting for me. For an instant, I caught his gaze. Guilt and shame surfaced, and I quickly looked away and focused on getting the car parked. I was too embarrassed to look up, so I pretended to look for something in the car. I didn't want to get out of the car, but I knew eventually I would have to and do this thing, whatever it was.

Oh, God, my heart was pounding. *What was I thinking by coming here? Were those clothes really worth this? What am I doing here?*

I had never had a panic attack, but I know the symptoms well. I was getting there real fast.

I took a couple of deep breaths, proceeded to take off my sunglasses, and whispered to myself, "This is it, baby," as I slowly opened the car door and stepped out.

* * *

The day had been laid out to allow more than enough time to visit with Allen. I had finished all of my errands. I had purposely allowed myself several hours to visit Allen, just in case things went well before I was expected to show up at a friend's home for the weekend.

I remembered Quem's advice. Start over with Allen—try it again. I felt determined to do this thing—to try again—but at the same time I knew I had options. I could very easily go down the street and go shopping until it was time to meet my friend.

When I stepped out of the car my legs felt wobbly, so I deliberately made myself take each step forward until I got closer to Allen. As I approached Allen, I noticed that he had backed up a little, ending up in front of his front door, facing me. Finally, I looked at Allen and our eyes met. Putting on a first-class show like everything was just fine, I gave him a smile. Only it wasn't just fine, and we both knew it. I said, "Hi."

Allen was eyeing my new punk hairstyle. I laughed and told him that Kaycie, my hairdresser, had begged me to trust her to try something new. I kind of liked it, but told him it would wash out.

He just laughed as he nodded his head and took another drag on his cigarette.

My hair was the least of my concerns. I saw that Allen had taken a protective stance, standing between me and his front door. *I certainly couldn't blame him.*

Yep, here it is. He isn't going to ask me in. But being me, I asked if I could come in to get my stuff. He shifted his body to make room for me to slide by and go in as he opened the door. Three feet inside the door, I saw my clothes draped over the back of a side chair.

Clearly, he had already painted the picture, and it looked like it had had plenty of time to dry. Allen was making it very easy for me to get my stuff and get out. However, that wasn't the way it all played out. After we got inside the door, I felt the maleness of him and I felt my heart open.

Inside, I was a mess. Outwardly, I expertly presented myself as level-headed and detached from his energy. Nonchalantly, I made the comment that he had my stuff all ready and politely thanked him. I stepped forward to pick my clothes up and began to go to the door. I felt like I had left my body—I was on automatic pilot. But somewhere deep inside I heard myself screaming, "Nakala what on Earth are you doing?" I ignored it.

Allen didn't sound condescending when he spoke, but I must have struck something in him, because he asked me if I were coming back *this* time. I just looked back at him and wondered if he really wanted me to come back. *Did he really know how much I loved him, yet I was clearly out of my element? My thoughts and feelings were in direct and utter conflict with one another concerning him.*

At that precise moment, Allen took the clothes from me and laid them back on the chair. He turned to face me, and I knew. He reached out for me and gently pulled me to him. I felt my body meld into his and we just held each other for a while. I wanted to be with him, but my thoughts slid back in time to when I was desperate and had lost control of my feelings and fled. In my mind I whispered, *Dear Father in heaven, what am I to do now?*

I was the first to pull away, but it was for a different reason than to leave. I looked up into his eyes and saw his acceptance and reached for his neck to pull him closer. I kissed him and he kissed back. I felt the soft pressure of his lips turn into desire. He knew.

Nathanal wanted me to look at this very closely and whispered, "Nakala, sweetheart, it is time for you to decide if you are going to work on this relationship or not. You can walk away right now and never look back if you want. It is your decision."

With all of my might, I pushed back my fear. Without saying a word, I saw Allen as he calmly stepped away from our embrace and turned to go up the stairs. My mind whirled and my body tingled.

His move away from me confused me; threw me off. I didn't understand what he was doing. My first thought was that he may be going to get something and would be right back. All of this was so out of character. I felt like I was being abandoned. I didn't like how I felt, so I asked him,

"Allen, where are you going?" Allen turned around to look at me long enough to say, "To my room. Are you coming?"

In my mind, I was engaged in a war of epic proportions. I knew that what I was about to do may not be wisest thing, but I kicked off my shoes anyway and followed him upstairs.

CHAPTER
EIGHT

During my stay in Kansas City I had casually told Nancy, the friend I was staying with, that I was planning a trip to Sedona in three weeks.

To my astonishment, upon hearing my announcement, Nancy became really excited and almost jumped out of her seat. Nancy works with her guides like I do. We both know when we are in alignment with Spirit. She quickly said, "Nakala, I have been pulled to be in Sedona during the Spring Equinox."

Quickly, we grabbed the calendar and looked at the date of the Spring Equinox and saw that I would be right there. This was one bit of information that *someone* had decided not to share with me.

Nancy, obviously, was supposed to be in Sedona at that time. However, she was concerned with the financial aspect of the trip.

Again, we both know that if you want to do something and it is for your highest good, the universe will provide the way.

All of this was confusing me, because I really thought I'd be making this trip alone. *What was it that Nathanal had told me? Did he specifically say that I'd be driving there alone? Perhaps I assumed that part…*

I reminded Nancy that I had a car that got forty plus miles to the gallon, and I'd be paying for that anyway. The drawback was that my car was small and would be full of enough of my belongings to get me through several weeks. I doubted that she would be comfortable. While Nancy and I were talking about our options, I was telepathically communicating with Nathanal. Several times, I asked him if she were to go with me. I just was having trouble believing what was happening. Every single time I heard him say the very same thing: "It is fine."

Then I remembered Ann, Nancy's closest friend, and asked, "Nancy, what about her? She *always* takes road trips with you." So what did Nancy do? Impromptu, Nancy picked up her cell phone and called her. They both were in.

We carefully looked at the logistics and wondered about the two of them driving out with me and then flying back. In my mind, I knew we couldn't get all of their stuff in my car and have room for them, too.

After checking flight costs, we decided to take two cars. It was perfect. The three of us could take turns driving. I was thinking one of us could take a break and rest. If we wanted to, we could drive alone and crank up the music.

It was decided. We would take two cars, leaving on Sunday, March 17. Nancy and Ann would stay until the end of the week in Sedona. From there I would drive on to Prescott and they would head back to Kansas.

The last thing to finalize was where we would meet. We decided that they would drive down to Wichita and meet me and go southwest from there. From Wichita, it looked like it would take us seventeen hours to get to Sedona.

Unfortunately, one week before we were to leave for Arizona I became ill. I had been in so much pain that I had decided to get an appointment with an MD. The doctor did some tests on me, told me I had a virus, prescribed some medicine, and sent me home with the words, "You'll be fine in time to make your trip to Sedona." I was looking at six days before I would leave.

Two days before our trip I had still been in pain, and a lot of it. Even so, somehow I managed to get my belongings packed and my car loaded.

I kept my friends up to speed on my illness, telling them I was not contagious but really was tired and very uncomfortable. I was upfront with them, telling them I honestly didn't know if I could make the trip or not. I also told them that Nathanal had never deviated from his game plan. We all remained hopeful and open to a positive outcome.

Nancy asked me to consult my guides for which route to take, which hotels to stay at, and which restaurants to eat at that would be for the highest good.

The date to leave was fast approaching and I wasn't feeling any better. Every day I'd wake up and assess my body for symptoms. Every day I asked Nathanal if we should stay home and nix the trip. Every day his response was always the same. "We are going. Know this. You will be fine." But I wasn't fine—I didn't feel good.

I kept wondering about the lesson I had been given earlier concerning taking care of the Temple of God—my body! The words I had been given over and over were, "The body must take you through your journey. You are responsible for it." It wasn't my aim to abuse my body. I questioned if any of this was logical, and then I remembered who I work with. (The guides think and work outside of the box. In other words, we as humans are very limited in solving our so-called problems.)

PART
TWO

ARIZONA

CHAPTER
NINE

Excitement was in the air—today was the day Nancy, Ann, and I would begin our journey to Sedona. My attitude was upbeat, and physically, I felt much better. I had more energy. My mantra of "Every day, in every way, I am getting better and better" was working.

I said a quick goodbye to my mother, and then I hit the road, heading down Interstate 35 to Park City (a suburb of Wichita) to meet Nancy and Ann.

We had a quick lunch—I could sense the anticipation each of us was feeling; we were ready to get on the road! I followed Nancy and Ann to Highway 54 and said farewell to Wichita. My enthusiasm dwindled as I took in the view. I saw an infinitely long, lonely stretch of concrete. There was not a tree in sight. About an hour into the trip, my body started to ache. Even though I knew I needed to rest, I forced myself to continue driving.

I drove for five hours that day, and when we finally stopped for the night, I was exhausted and in an excruciating amount of pain. All I really wanted to do was to curl up into a tight ball and cry, but instead I held all my emotions in check. No one knew how I was really feeling—physically or emotionally. Again, I wondered what the wisdom was in taking this trip.

After breakfast the next morning, the journey continued. Fifteen minutes into the drive, I broke down and began to sob uncontrollably. I simply was unable to stop.

Finally, I heard Nathanal say, "Nakala." He waited a few seconds and said my name again louder, with more emphasis, "NA-KA-LA!" I could not respond.

Then I heard Nathanal command me to get my phone and call Nancy. I couldn't even do that. I was in agony—I could barely reach over to grab my phone. But Nathanal did not give up on me. Repeatedly, he told me to get my phone and call my friends. I finally summoned the strength to reach over to pick up my phone. I hit call, and after a few rings I heard Nancy answer on the other end. As soon as Nancy heard my voice, she said, "Nakala, you see that turn off up there? Pull over!" I didn't drive another mile the entire trip, and I know that I would not have made it to Sedona without Nancy and Ann.

On Tuesday, in the midafternoon, we arrived in Sedona. The city was hot, dusty, and buzzing with activity. The traffic was bumper to bumper. The sidewalks were crowded with people. Perplexed, I asked, "Ann, why are there so many people here?" In a matter-of-fact tone, Ann answered, "This is the week of the Spring Equinox and there are several workshops and meditations scheduled."

My heart felt heavy as I thought about the difficulty we would probably have finding rooms. When we had first begun to talk about this trip I had envisioned March being a month that would be fairly quiet. I was so wrong.

The impact hit me hard. I whispered to Nathanal that I hoped he knew what he was doing. I heard him laugh in response to my statement. Even though I had been relieved of my driving duties, I didn't feel any better. It was getting more difficult for me to put on a happy face.

Even so, it was time for me to work with Nathanal and find us a place to stay while we were here. Having the responsibility to find a place to stay was making me feel stressed. I felt like it was all up to me. I had to remind myself that Nathanal was here and he would find us the perfect place. All I had to do was listen to him and relay the messages to Nancy and Ann.

Nathanal had us first stop at a very small motel to check rates. I noticed that the parking lot encompassing the front of the motel looked unkempt, with weeds growing from the cracks in the asphalt and piles of dirt and sand here and there. There was no vegetation of any sort to give the feeling of home.

When I walked into the reception area, I immediately felt claustrophobic. The place had a dusty, dirty feel to it, and I coughed as I took in a breath.

I estimated the laminated desk was a mere ten feet from the dirty glass front door, which left little room for more than one person. Currently, the clerk was assisting another customer, which left me more than enough time to check out the place. Trying to stay objective, I felt the energy of the two men and the room. Nathanal wanted me to find out the rates. He also wanted me to *feel* the energy.

I felt it all right and I was reacting to it! I wanted out of there quickly. But it seemed I was committed to stay, because here I was in line to talk to the clerk. I didn't want to be rude and just walk out the door before I at least spoke to the man.

I fidgeted. The room was hot. To distract me from my discomfort, I scanned the tiny reception room to find something that would hold my interest until it was my turn to speak to the clerk. On the desk I noticed an arrangement of old, faded plastic flowers in a worn wicker basket. I was not impressed. *How many years have those flowers been there? Who originally put them there? They should have been discarded years ago. Did his wife die? Maybe he just does not have any taste.*

When my turn finally came to talk to the clerk, I asked what the rate was for a room with two queen beds. The room was affordable. So I asked the next question. "Do you have one available for tonight?" Even without looking at his records he said, "No."

Well that was huge relief because I would not have wanted to stay there anyway. I politely thanked him, turned, and walked out.

As I walked to the cars I wondered how many places Nathanal would take us to before we found something.

After I told Ann and Nancy that they didn't have a room, Ann and I drove on down the street with Nancy following us until Nathanal instructed me to pull in to another parking lot. This time the place was completely opposite in appearance from the last place. The landscape was exotic and well-manicured, with palm trees, cacti, and other succulent plants strategically placed to have the maximum effect to please, no matter the cost.

The large parking lot had been recently resurfaced, with nice, clean yellow stripes to guide the flow of their guests. The stucco and stone building was up-scale, with a water feature centrally located. A nice finishing touch was the black wrought iron fencing and gates that divided the parking lot from the courtyard.

The sign outside had been erected on a stone foundation that was quite attractive and accented with a nice collection of red and white azaleas in full bloom. Yup, I figured this place might be a little on the pricy side.

Not expecting an answer, I asked, "My Nathanal, oh, what are you up to?" I could tell just by the signage that it was going to be more than I was prepared to spend. We pulled into the parking lot, found two spaces, and parked. Ann and I went in. Nancy said she wanted to wait for us outside.

The lobby was incredibly busy, and we had to wait for several minutes before we were assisted. As I stood there waiting at the desk, I began to notice details. The clerks wore navy blue slacks with red tops and metallic gold name tags.

On a cloth-covered table, over by the wall, they had coffee with creamer and sugar and freshly baked chocolate chip cookies. Beside the table stood a large ice-filled container with coke products and bottled water. Nice touch, I thought.

I began to fret over what was happening and played back the facts as I saw them. Was this a lesson in learning to value myself enough to stay in a nice place? However, Nancy was on a tight budget. Heck, I was on a budget! Nancy didn't come in to give her opinion, and it was up to me to say yea or nay.

The receptionist informed us that they had only one room available for one night. Intuitively, I knew that we should stay there for the night and just enjoy ourselves. However, after specials and taxes, the price of the room was roughly three hundred dollars. It was up to me to make the final decision, and to make it for someone else took me way out of my comfort zone.

When the receptionist quoted the room rate, Ann and I exchanged looks, trying not to look conspicuous. I felt my energy shift. Personally, I didn't want to spend $100 (my share) for one night. I still had several weeks of unknown expenses looking me straight in the face.

Ann looked me square in the eyes and told me flat out, "I don't care about the money. We can't take it with us." Then she so wisely added, "You know, your guides will keep creating situations like this until you give up this insecurity concerning money. You have to surrender, Nakala."

I looked at her and nodded my head that I knew that she was correct, but all the while my head was swimming with uncertainty. Oh, yes, I knew that my guides would keep creating scenarios that would create fear until I overcame it. Then I heard myself tell the clerk that we would take the room in a voice that sounded much stronger than I felt.

The room was wonderful—first class all of the way. Two king-size beds, with spreads and accenting drapes made of brocade silk patterned fabric incorporating rich hues of reds, browns, and gold. I was drawn in to the design by a slight shimmer of metallic thread, woven in to impress.

The bath was huge—with a Jacuzzi tub and a shower with two shower-heads. I thought how romantic the shower would be for couples—then thought of Allen…

The walls, floor, and fixtures were a gold-veined black marble. Everything was highly polished, reflecting the lights that gave the room a lovely glow. There were handmade soaps, shampoos, conditioners, razors, and other accessories set out to make our stay more comfortable. On a side table were more than enough plush white towels. In addition, the hotel even provided bathrobes and slippers for their guests. We were more than comfortable. I whispered my thanks to Nathanal for giving me this gift and saw him nod his head to acknowledge that he heard me.

We brought in our belongings and began to unwind and get down to business concerning what we wanted to accomplish during our stay in Sedona. Since I had never been to Sedona before, I wanted to learn the layout of the city. It was still early and Ann said she wanted to go find the Welcome Center and get some literature on the area for day hikes and places to visit that would interest all of us. Nancy wanted to stay at the hotel and rest.

Ann and I both thought it would be a good idea to look around and see if we could find another place to stay for the next two nights. So we left Nancy to enjoy her time alone.

We found the Welcome Center and Ann casually mentioned to the attendant about looking for a place to stay for the following two nights. Well, I am told there are no coincidences. The woman behind the desk said, "I know of the perfect place. Let me tell you about it."

While Ann talked with the greeter, I talked with Nathanal about the hotel that Ann was getting the low-down on. Nathanal said, "Call them and get the details. I believe you will be most pleased."

We walked out of the Welcome Center with a handful of brochures and a definite possibility for a place to stay. I was beginning to feel better already.

CHAPTER
TEN

e drove around town for a while and made mental notes about some restaurants that we'd like to try out and where some interesting shops were, then headed back to the hotel.

We ate our fresh veggies, crackers, and hummus for dinner and then we all got ready for bed. No one turned on the TV. *These are my kind of people.*

The following day we had agreed to get in a morning hike before the sun had its say and heated up the place. But beforehand, we headed over to the hotel to take a look at what we had booked and confirm our reservation for the next two nights. Our room wasn't quite as nice as the one we had just stayed at, but it had a fantastic view of the mountains. We were also in the heart of town. All of the stores and restaurants were within walking distance. No more fighting traffic or looking for a parking space. We could check in at 3 that afternoon.

We were ready to tackle our first hike…at Bell Rock. There was talk about going to Cathedral Rock and some other places after our first hike. I listened to the plans, hating to put a damper on them by how I felt physically, so I didn't. I bit my lip and wondered how I would do on this hike. I silently prayed it would be a very short adventure.

We arrived at Bell Rock to find the u-shaped parking lot quite large, with very few empty spaces left. We had to drive to the very end to find a space. The heat had already set in. We all grabbed our water bottles, cameras, and phones.

Hiking around Bell Rock proved to be an all-uphill battle. I knew right away that I had made a huge error by agreeing to come, but kept walking anyway for a while. For some time my mantra was, "Surely we will turn around any moment."

However, after walking probably half a mile, I knew that I had to own up to my mistake, and I told Ann and Nancy that I was going to stop there for a while, then head back to the starting point and wait for them there.

I saw an area off the main path that seemed secluded, and I looked for a place to sit and rest. The red Sedona soil was nothing like the black earth we have in Kansas. In Sedona the soil has more sand in it, yet it is like powder—a red powder that blows everywhere. The area was heavily littered with rocks of all sizes and shapes.

For my rest, I imagined a rock that looked like a chair, with a slight curve to its seat and a back to support me. I figured there had to be one around here, but no such luck. Instead, I found a twenty-foot long ledge that faced the east with a beautiful view. There wasn't anyone else around, so I sat down to just be in the energy of this beautiful place.

Instead of being alone in a quiet, reflective space, though, a Mexican woman from Colorado meandered by and decided to join me while she waited for her kids to come back down from the rock. We ended up talking for a good fifteen minutes about her many hiking trips across the country.

After our visit, I headed back to the starting point—each step reminding me that I should have been wiser with my choice. Finally, I saw the stone shelter (a solid rock wall with several stone posts supporting the roof). The wall displayed a detailed map of the area. I hadn't even noticed the map before and noted that it sure would have been helpful had I seen what I was in for before I took off.

There were people everywhere—no quiet place for me to lie down and let loose all the pent up frustration and pain. I was so tired of acting like I felt good. I wanted to become small—invisible. Working to see the positive, I made note of the two stone benches for people to rest on—they were hard and unyielding, but at least there was a place to sit down. I would be in partial shade and somewhat protected from the wind.

Negativity came flooding back to me, and all I could think about was how exhausted and dehydrated I was. I touched my lips—they were dry and beginning to crack from the combination of sun and wind. *I want to get into Ann's car to get my ChapStick. I want to get into Ann's car and leave.*

While I waited for Ann and Nancy to return, I sipped my bottled water. Not knowing how long I would have to wait, I worked to make my water last as long as possible and saw that I could amuse myself by offering to take pictures for a few groups. The time went by very, very slowly.

In between group pictures I thought about my situation—surmising that while I was here in Sedona there would be no more walks or shopping for me. If possible I'd stay in the hotel while the others did their thing. *What was going on in my physical body?* I felt immense fear rise as I thought about it. *Something's not right in my body. Oh, God, what is wrong with me?*

Under normal circumstances, I might have been upset…even jealous that I could not join the group and hike, but this time there was nothing left in me to feel. All I wanted was to ease the pain. I was that tired. A tear slipped down my sunburnt cheek. Quickly, I brushed it away, hoping no one would notice.

My guides know what they are doing. They brought me here for a reason.

CHAPTER
ELEVEN

When I awoke the next morning, the first thing I noticed was the stunning view from our patio. I immediately said a prayer of gratitude and felt my spirits lift.

The girls headed out early, while I slept for several more hours. Every so often I would get up to snack on some raw veggies and hummus. Finally, there was no more sleep, and I began to feel a little trapped and alone.

Nathanal directed me to get out the Evergreen Club directory that he had told me to bring along. (Evergreen is an international club offering homes to stay at, costing very little.) I got out the booklet and looked for the Arizona page. Luckily there were eight members in Prescott. Still, this was extremely short notice. *Would I be able to find someone who would take us?*

The first call I made was to a woman named Gloria. She wasn't home. On her message she sounded older. I left a message for her to call me back and went to the next person on the list.

The other seven were either out of town, sick, or had a death in the family. I didn't have a choice but to wait for Gloria to call me back. So I got on the computer and began to look up cabin rentals and made one call. I was getting a little nervous that I didn't have any definite plans on where to stay. That evening I told the girls about all the calls I had made and still was in limbo. Our plan was to leave on our separate paths sometime Friday.

Suddenly, seemingly out of the clear blue sky, Nancy announced, "We will be driving you to Prescott." I was stunned. I couldn't process what she had told me. So I asked, "What?" In an annoying sort of way, Nancy slowed her words down and raised the pitch of her voice, "We will drive you to Prescott."

Prescott was another two hours further southwest from Sedona, through mountainous terrain, and completely out of their way. Still, I wasn't able to comprehend what I had heard. I began to make a mental list of all the reasons why they should *not* do this thing for me: their time, gas (which was $3.70 per gallon), extra mileage and wear and tear on Ann's car, additional expenses for hotels and food.

Guilt was creeping in. I reasoned that what was being offered was unnecessary, and even on the brink of being absurd. I did not want to be a bother, nor did I want to cost them extra money. I swallowed hard, looked at both Nancy and Ann, and heard myself ask, "Nancy, it is way out of your way to do this. Are you sure?" She told me in a voice that left no room for argument. "I must take you to Prescott to make sure you get there—last time you didn't."

CHAPTER
TWELVE

I felt a movement in my chest like something had hit me. My breath caught. I didn't question Nancy's statement. Instead, I connected with Nathanal and asked him, "What is going on? Why didn't I get to Prescott the first time? Is this some sort of a karmic thing?"

I heard him say, "Nakala, allow them this gift."

Part of me wanted to know why Nancy felt that she must take me all the way to Prescott. Never once did I consider that this was simply an incredible act of kindness. Instead, I assumed that she was paying back some sort of karma.

My guess was that I probably died en route to Prescott during a previous lifetime, and well…I decided it wasn't worth my effort to ask any more questions—at least not now. I didn't have any spare energy to use on the formulation of questions or the process of sifting through any data. I wasn't sure it even mattered. If one of my guides thought it would benefit me to know about this past life, they would surely talk to me about it at some point.

Over the years, I have found that everything my guides do is for a reason and that it is usually best if I allow them to reveal information when they are ready. Anyway, I just didn't have the energy to work on the reasons why Nancy was so sure that she was to get me to Prescott this time.

My phone rang, taking me from my thoughts. I looked at the caller ID and saw it was an Arizona area code. Oh, I so hoped this was the woman that I had left a message with. To my amazement, it was!

I began to explain to Gloria that I was traveling to Prescott the next day with my two friends and we needed a place to stay. One night's stay for all of us and then an extended stay for me until I found a more permanent place. Gloria asked where we were from and if she could help me find a place. Shaking my head in disbelief I answered, "That is so kind of you, and yes, I could use some help. Thank you." She was more than accommodating. We were set.

Finding a place in Prescott had been a tedious affair. I had made nine calls to Prescott. That process had come full circle, with us staying with the very first person I called. I had to laugh. Sure would be nice, I thought, if Nathanal would tell me, "Hey, Nakala, Gloria's your gal," in the first place, "and by the way Nakala, Nancy and Ann will take you there." Anyway, we had a place overnight that was safe, clean, and economical!

The plan was that I would stay at Gloria's over the weekend while I looked for a more permanent place, while Nancy and Ann would leave first thing Saturday morning, after breakfast.

All along I knew that my friends would have to leave soon, but I didn't want to think of that and I certainly didn't want to feel the fear of being alone there, so I knowingly pushed it all down, avoiding the inevitable.

When I agreed to stay at Gloria's, I felt myself slip into the fear of being left in a strange place. This time I recognized what I was doing and quickly disengaged. Then I told myself, "Now, Nakala, you have come this far." I affirmed that everything was going to work out for the highest good. Then I began to breathe to relax.

Gloria lived near the very top of Thumb Butte and had a beautiful home with a view that was certainly a gift straight from God.

Gloria was extremely gracious and told me that I could certainly stay there until I had secured a house in the area suitable for my needs. Her price was more than fair, so I agreed to stay until Monday. I figured that surely I'd find a place by then. I certainly didn't want to take advantage of her hospitality.

Saturday morning was bittersweet—a chapter finished. When I woke up I felt as if I were outside of my body, watching myself interact with everyone from a distance. I knew I was speaking to everyone…I could hear myself; it just didn't feel real. It was like being in shock—just going through the motions minus the feelings. It was really strange to be in two places at once.

Logically, I knew that my friends were due to head out soon, leaving me in Gloria's home. I knew that if I allowed myself to ponder my situation I may panic. Instead, I intentionally focused on the facts that I was not only safe in this home but was in the presence of a kindred spirit.

The four of us enjoyed a lovely breakfast, with a wide variety of fresh fruit and pastries served on crystal dishes. We ate from dishes of fine china with linen napkins. Gloria offered juice, milk, and coffee—it was a lovely way to begin my stay.

The breakfast area was hexagonal in shape and was located on the southwest corner of the house, with three over-size windows giving us full view of three directions. To the south, we could see a beautiful wooded valley, bordered by a mountain range. To the west, we could see more houses and an array of giant rocks of all shapes and sizes, and to the north was the top of Thumb Butte, which was like a colossal rock that someone evidently thought looked like a thumb. So far, I hadn't seen the resemblance—maybe I could from a different direction.

Gloria had opened the window shades to get full benefit of the morning light and to enjoy her view of the surrounding area. She mentioned that there were mule deer around and wild hogs. When I stopped to think of this place and me in it…well, I knew that this was truly a blessing. *Well, Nathanal, you got me here. Don't know why, but here I am!*

After breakfast, we all said our goodbyes. When I hugged my friends, a part of me wanted to hang on for dear life, but a bigger part of me said, *You are a grown woman—act like one. Your time has come. It is time to move on.*

CHAPTER
THIRTEEN

Finding a place to rent took a lot of work. On Saturday I brainstormed, using all the resources that I knew to be available. First thing I did was get on the Internet and find property management companies in the area.

The very first company I saw was called Prescott Cabin Rentals. The website was well developed and interesting. I clicked on the links to view some of the properties listed. There were a few houses that looked good, but the prices were more than I wanted to pay. I decided to contact the company anyway. There wasn't an answer, so I left a message.

Gloria had suggested that I visit the Chamber of Commerce downtown on the square, so I did. The people were nice enough, but weren't really able to help me.

For several hours I drove around, looking for addresses for apartments. Nothing I saw resonated with me. I looked at the time and saw that Saturday was shot! I had spent the entire day driving around Prescott, figuring out the street layout and looking for places that would help me secure a house or an apartment, with no luck.

Monday morning was coming fast and I was beginning to get a bit frustrated. I hadn't found a place and I was feeling the pain more than ever. I reprimanded myself for pushing myself so hard. On the way back to

Gloria's home, I looked for hotels that might be possibilities if I couldn't find a permanent place by Monday.

Gloria's personality seemed to be the business/motherly type. When I got back to her place, she asked me a number of questions regarding my process of finding a place to stay. All I could do was walk her through my steps, telling her what I had done so far. She offered me some sound advice, gave me an area map, phone numbers, and pulled out her yellow pages and her newspaper.

After looking through the resources that she offered, I realized that I was out of ideas. I had struck out on finding a small, furnished apartment or cabin. I began to wonder about the possibility of looking for a roommate. I picked up the newspaper and found one ad. Not having any other leads at the moment, I found my phone, called the number, and got a recorded message. The voice was a female, and that crumb gave me a tiny bit of hope. I left a message, then I checked the yellow pages for furnished apartments.

It was then that Nathanal stepped in to caution me. "Nakala, do not rent a place where you will be sharing space with anyone. During this stay you require your privacy and a place that will serve all of your needs. You will be preparing most of your meals."

My phone rang, interrupting me from receiving anything else from Nathanal. I looked at the number to see if I recognized it. No, but it was an Arizona area code. Maybe it was one of those companies that I had left messages at. Ah! It *was* Prescott Cabin Rentals! My hopes soared.

The woman identified herself as Wendy. After I explained that I would be staying for a minimum of four weeks, Wendy decided that I may be interested in looking at a couple of cabins that she rented out long-term. She immediately got my e-mail address and sent me the photos and rates. I liked what I saw but still wasn't sure I should commit, and I e-mailed her back saying that I wanted to look at them in person. We made an appointment to meet at the cabins on Sunday morning.

Sunday was quickly upon me. Once again, I joined Gloria for breakfast and immediately saw that she hadn't deviated from her first class service. The aroma and flavor of the coffee was so delicious that I asked her what brand it was, making a mental note to buy some when I got myself settled.

Together we enjoyed the morning view and discussed how she ended up in Prescott. As I looked out the window I saw five mule deer, partially hidden by the boulders and bushes. I could see they were being very cautious before crossing the street.

My body reminded me in a very loud voice that I should rest, but I knew that I had that appointment with Wendy to see the cabins. I knew if that didn't work out I would have to really hustle.

After I got myself ready for the day, I walked to my car and entered in the address in my GPS. I headed down Thumb Butte Mountain towards the east and then south out of Prescott into Prescott Valley, passing all of the same retailers and restaurants that I was familiar with in Kansas.

There were two cabins to see that were side by side like a duplex. One was decorated in a Victorian style with antiques and the other had more of a country feel to it, also sprinkled with antiques.

I liked the cabins but just wasn't sure, so I told Wendy that I'd call her back. Nothing else I did panned out.

After two days of research and several hours in my car learning my way around Prescott, I felt like I was just plain done. My body screamed at me. "Listen to me! I am in PAIN! Please let me rest." But I couldn't rest. I had to find a place.

I found Gloria's address on my GPS and headed back to her house. I hadn't found anything any better or more economical than the very first cabin I had looked at on the Internet. Again, I had come full circle.

The fatigue did not let up and the time in the car looking for streets and addresses had left its toll on me. I was spent. I decided to rest for the remainder of the day and wait before I made a decision. There were still a few calls that I expected to have returned on properties. But since it was Sunday I figured I may have to wait until Monday before I heard anything definite. At this point, taking a nap sounded really good. This illness thing was really causing me some anxiety. *What is wrong with me?*

There wasn't any outward indication that there was anything wrong with me. The pain in my abdomen caused not only physical stress but mental and emotional as well. The pain rarely let up and really messed with my level of energy. All I wanted to do was lay down. I worried about my health. *I'm not better…the doctor must have misdiagnosed me.*

Even though I was concerned about my health, I felt that this thing, whatever it was, had in a way been a huge blessing for me. I was able to look at other people with a different attitude—no judgment. Until now, I had not thought about how people can be really ill, but not outwardly show any signs of illness. In other words, there are reasons people maneuver through their days the way they do, and those reasons I have no way of knowing.

This illness had also shown me that constant pain is a very significant stressor, often changing the way people conduct their lives. Not having the energy to do ordinary things like going shopping for groceries, cleaning the house, or even bathing can easily throw a person into a depression. In addition, chronic pain may be a downward spiral, manifesting more illnesses.

Interrupting my analysis of the condition of man, I heard Nathanal say, "Please get your journal." My journal was beside me, so all I had to do was pick it up and open it. Done deal.

"I'm ready, Nathanal."

"My dear Nakala, we have brought you to this place for a multitude of reasons. We specifically brought you to Prescott so you would stay put. Had we instructed you to go to a place, say Oklahoma City, that was near your home in Kansas, I dare say you would have gotten in your car and driven home. We needed you to be in one place for a fair length of time in order to receive.

"When I speak of receiving, it is quite a broad topic. You were promised that you would receive the gift to channel a book from Samuel Paul. Now, your priorities have possibly shifted? Perhaps you would rather receive healing?

"For you, I ask, Nakala, what is more important, to receive the writings or healing?"

For me, there was no question! I didn't need to think about it. Having the gift of a healthy body far exceeded anything else I could imagine having right now.

"Nakala, in order to heal in entirety, you must change your ways. I shall clarify my meaning. Your thoughts and emotions have caused your illness. For years you have lived with particular beliefs that did not benefit you—so much so, that you have begun to manifest blocks (misalignment of spirit) in your physical tissue. What I speak of is that your belief is you feel you are not worthy to be assisted, treated fairly, or even loved by another.

"You have lived almost your entire life in fear of persecution. Dear one, it is all an illusion, nothing but a belief that you created eons ago that was renewed this lifetime; all too easily, I might add."

Nathanal continued, "Father Quem came and taught on this very subject. How well do you recall his words? Your very own thoughts and emotions have made you ill. We have brought you here to work with you to change your beliefs and habits. It is your time to do this. It's well past time, Nakala."

Nathanal continued on, "Because of the emotion of fear, you have held tight your lower body (constricting the flow of energy) in areas such as your abdomen. This is an involuntary action on your part in the defense of some sort of imaginary oncoming blow, be it verbal or of a physical nature. Nakala, you are safe now.

"Nevertheless, on a subtle level you have held those beliefs—those thoughts which created emotion. Those emotions caused masses of dense energy in your etheric bodies, followed by your physical body. Quite simply, up to this juncture in your life you have not yet received the full knowledge to show you what you have been creating in your physical reality.

"Nakala, you have worked with us on a conscious level now for several years. During this time we have given you many teachings. It has also been our pleasure to give you the opportunity to channel our words, our teachings to others. This trip to Arizona is to finalize your lessons in preparation for what is to come.

"When we travel home, back to Kansas, you are to finalize arrangements and prepare for your physical move back to Kansas City. Our work together is nearing. Your placement must be secure. Do you hear me, Nakala?"

I didn't answer Nathanal right away. I couldn't. Even though I had known for some time that I would be returning to the Kansas City area, to hear Nathanal tell me it was time caused me a multitude of emotions.

I was torn. This meant it was time for me to leave the area where my elderly mother and father were. I had known for some time that it was only a matter of when, but I still was unable to grasp that it was finally time. I finally managed to get my voice back. "Yes, Nathanal, I hear you."

Nathanal wasn't finished. He calmly told me, "Call Wendy and tell her that you'll take the cabin—the one with the white wicker furniture."

CHAPTER
FOURTEEN

It seemed to me that I had come a long way with my work with the beings of light since I began to hear them speak to me and through me. For some time now I had followed their directives. I had learned to trust my guides, the Pleiadians, enough to travel long distances for reasons initially unknown to me.

I'd hoped to write a book while I was in Arizona, but obviously, that wasn't the most important reason for me to be there. I was there to learn to love myself. I really thought I did.

Monday morning I moved into the charming cabin with the white wicker furniture, with the perk of having a canyon in my back yard. Then I drove to Walmart, Kmart, and Trader Joe's for supplies and food.

I was settled for the most part and working to familiarize myself with where everything was. The sounds were different here and I wondered if tonight I would be afraid to go to bed.

There was a scratching sound over by the side window. I just wanted to rest, but the sound was distracting. I looked up and saw that it was nearing dusk. I hadn't realized the time had slipped by so quickly. I got up to check the noise and found that it was only a limb scraping against the windowpane. The room was really getting dark.

A chill had settled in the room, so I decided to get up and find a sweater. As I got up, I saw the sky had shifted from its former self to a gloomy dark gray. Maybe we would get some rain. I thought about the trees that were beginning to bud and wondered if the canyon would take on a more vibrant green once they received the moisture they required.

Nathanal had brought me here to see one of God's fantastic creations—one that was foreign to me. For some reason, the scene took me to an intimate place. I felt a sense of serenity.

The view I had was nothing compared to what I saw in Kansas. Here in Arizona my back yard was a canyon that looked to be at first glance an unruly mess of gray-green vegetation. The soil was sandy with a reddish tint and there were rocks and boulders of all colors and sizes, sprinkled everywhere with dots of cacti, cedar trees, tufts of dead grass and other scruffy plants unknown to me. Everything was wild, unkempt.

In Kansas, my back yard (which was utterly flat) joined another back yard, also flat. At this moment at home my crayon-green lawn was lush. It looked alive and manicured. The rose bushes, clematis, tulips, and daffodils would be blooming, providing a wide variety of color, texture, and scent. I felt a stab of melancholy. *I miss my family and friends. I miss my home. I miss Allen.*

My guides knew exactly what they were doing when they brought me here.

Again my thoughts were interrupted, only this time it was Samuel Paul. He was saying, "I'd like to give you words just now, if you don't mind, Nakala." I hadn't realized that I was crying until I heard my voice break when I told him I'd get his book and sit down.

"Nakala, you have been gifted much by answering the call to come here. The journey was a difficult one for you, and I know without the assistance of your two friends it would have been impossible for you to make it. Your mindset simply wouldn't have allowed you to continue.

"You, I am sure, would have found a way to get back home soon after that first day of travel. All was in alignment for you to have those willing to drive you here, and to your amazement they did!

"Nathanal, your personal guide, planned this retreat for you for many reasons. But to bring back your memory that you love yourself is the highest priority. You know, Nakala, you once loved yourself very much.

"The book I promised you will come when all is in alignment to do so." Although I knew the wisdom of what he was saying, I felt a deep sense of frustration and disappointment rise at the prospect of not writing while I was here.

Samuel Paul continued, "Your time here has just begun. You will be learning to establish a new routine, as well as learning to go through the day without the company of other human beings.

"Being alone is nothing new for you. However, to be in an environment that is foreign to this extent is a challenge for you. At the present moment you do not know the location of many of the facilities that will serve you for your coming days here. Recognize that you are creating stress because you are venturing into the future of the unknown. Watch your thoughts and emotions. Work to remain in the now, please."

For some reason, I felt like I had to defend myself. "Samuel Paul, I traveled to Italy alone. I experienced a definite language barrier, making travel difficult. Coming to Arizona seems like a piece of cake to me."

I wanted to say more, but as soon as I paused to gather my energy, Samuel Paul took control of the conversation. "May I remind you that every situation is different and is placed before you as a teaching?

"You were guided to Italy to learn to maneuver the modalities of travel: airplane, taxi, bus, and train. These were major fears of yours, and it was extremely stressful for you to buy tickets and to make sure you were where you needed to be for departure and knew how to find your way back. All without having the peace of mind that is found by receiving a confirmation from another living soul who spoke English to assure you that were on the right track. You were sent to Italy for many reasons, but the most important teaching at that time was to overcome the fear of traveling alone.

"This trip to Arizona is a little different, in the way that you are not working to overcome the fear of travel. Instead, this time you are working to overcome a fear of not being worthy to receive assistance from others. Sometimes these 'others' are people you have not before met in this lifetime.

"I will add that this opportunity has been given to you for another reason, and that is to overcome the fear of *asking* for assistance.

"For example, on the morning of the second day of travel coming here, shortly after getting in your car, you experienced an emotional breakdown.

"On that particular morning, you did not assess your energy properly. Instead, after a quick breakfast you promptly jumped in your car, as Ann and Nancy jumped in theirs. None of you asked the others what would work for the highest good.

"After just a few short minutes, you felt your energy plummet. The pain was fierce and you began to cry uncontrollably. The tears streamed down your face and the sobs, well…we all heard you and we all felt your discomfort—your agony, Nakala.

"We saw that you were mentally paralyzed with an outpouring of emotion, making it impossible for you to call for help.

"Nathanal made it known to you that you were to call Ann and Nancy for assistance. Several times Nathanal used the directive, "Nakala, call your friends." What was it that kept you from getting your phone and calling your friends to ask for help?"

My memory of the incident had left its mark and was still painfully fresh. I didn't want to think back and *feel* the despair once again, but I did as I was directed.

I began by saying, "That day I was exhausted, and I remember working hard to suppress the pain that I felt. But that wasn't all of it. It wasn't just about the pain or not having the energy I needed. Somehow, I felt like I didn't deserve to have their help! They had already done so much for me, and without me even asking! I didn't want them… I stopped speaking. I was shocked to finally realize how I truly felt—what stopped me from picking up the phone.

In a single instant it all became so crystal clear to me. I didn't feel good enough to have this type of support given to me.

"Samuel Paul, the feelings of guilt are surfacing. I felt guilty to ask and I felt guilty to receive!

"As I look back on that day there was a lot there that stopped me from picking up the phone. I was in pain and was crying pretty much uncontrollably. I felt frozen, unable to move, even though I was driving my car. I know that I didn't want my friends to see me in that state. I was very vulnerable and distraught. I was way out of control.

"In the past, in so many circumstances, I have swallowed hard my feelings and presented myself like nothing got to me. With my children, after my oldest son had passed on I felt like I had to be strong—stoic—to carry the family. In essence, I was the responsible one. But I guess hiding my feelings began way before I had children. There is a pattern to this. I see it now.

"Samuel Paul, as I think about this, I think the real reason might be that I didn't want anyone to see that I was vulnerable, because that would be like admitting that I am not strong enough to care for myself and am ultimately inferior to them. Oh, God, here we go again." I felt the emotions of sadness and grief well up and my tears threatened to spill over.

"Samuel Paul, I don't want to feel this way—like I am exposed, raw... literally stripped naked for all to see. Instead, I want to be one of *those* people who have it all figured out, but I am not."

I felt like I may be beginning to understand why I had broken down that day and maybe that would help me to understand myself a little better.

I stopped for a few moments and gathered my thoughts before I spoke again. "I work with you, Samuel Paul, and the other guides to help others. I feel like I must understand every nuance of myself—why I do certain things. If I don't understand myself then I won't understand anyone else."

Samuel Paul cut in then, "You work with us and for us, yes. Honestly, Miss, it is much easier to see the subtle energies in others than it is in yourself. In those cases when you are assisting another you are objective, as it is *their* lesson; they own it, not you. In addition, you always check in with the beings of light that you are working with before you ever offer advice. I know this to be fact.

"You are still in the human body, and because of this, ego is always there fighting for control. This ego fellow certainly has a strong desire to be in charge. However, it is time that you listen to your heart and allow your Higher Self to take control. The best way to do this is to stay in a state of detachment—never set before you a perceived outcome."

Suddenly, I felt a shift in energy and knew that Samuel Paul was about to change the subject.

"This brings me to another subject." Samuel Paul said.

I felt my heart grow heavy because I sensed where he was going to go with this. I heard myself sigh and let go.

"As I was saying, this brings me to another subject. This has to do with your friend, Allen. It would do you well to lay down *your* vision of a 'Happily Ever After.' Do you understand, Nakala?"

All I could say was, "I have a pretty good idea where you are going with this."

Samuel Paul channeled a breath through me, signaling me to relax and bring myself back to center before he began his message. "When you were told that you were to join with Allen, you naturally assumed because of your belief system that you would join in marriage with this one."

I cut him off then, my voice rising in protest—in anger—revealing my feelings of betrayal, "You all told me that!"

"Yes, we did," Samuel Paul agreed. "However, your vision of marriage differs a bit from ours. In your mind, you saw the two of you committing to living together for the rest of your days on this Earth. But your vision of the man you are to marry doesn't even come close to your present reality with Allen.

"Your perfect mate loves you and romances you with beautiful bouquets of flowers, taking you to dinner and to different events. This man whispers sweet nothings in your ear and opens the car door for you.

"In your mind, you see several areas of your relationship with Allen. Even though he states plainly that he loves you, what you have with him is in no way congruent with your way of romantic notions. Allen does not work a conventional job, and he has a daughter which he takes care of every weekend.

"In addition, he lives with his mother. Need I go further? When you were told that the two of you would join as a couple, all of your preconceived beliefs about your future husband literally flew out the window— what you wanted in and from your future husband was stolen...by us!

"You grew angry and did everything possible to change this situation to your preconceived favor. Time and time again you broke off your relationship with Allen, and to your utter amazement and dismay you were brought back together again and again.

"I dare say, when your relationship with Allen was renewed, you were in sheer bliss. All the while, your heart was telling you that the time spent with Allen was to prepare you for the shift to fifth dimensional consciousness. In order to ascend to this level, you must let go of what your lower consciousness or ego has worked to build (those preconceived ideations) in your mind.

"As your guides, we are highly evolved beings of light. We are able to see every conceivable angle to your development. We know how your mind works to protect itself by going into fear with every little illusionary threat to the ego.

"You have agreed with Allen on a higher level of awareness to work with him on this level to finalize your teachings to learn to control the ego self. We are excited to be a part of this journey.

"Nakala, I'd like to continue, if I may?" Samuel Paul was being rather formal today.

I felt a smile come across my face as my heart warmed. "Yes, Samuel Paul, please continue."

"Good! I didn't want to continue if you were losing interest, Nakala."

I paused and said, "Well, of course I am interested!"

Samuel Paul interjected, "I feel your energy and it wanes a bit. It would be best if we lay down our conversation for today. Perhaps we will pick it up again tomorrow?"

"Samuel Paul," I hesitated for a second before going forward with my question. "Why can't I see you?"

Samuel Paul spoke with authority, "Nakala, you are in the process of receiving a higher awareness that heightens senses. Stop typing now and look about you. Use your senses to detect another life form in your living space. Close your eyes if you must. Use your inner awareness. What do you sense?"

Samuel Paul's idea sounded like fun, so I did as he suggested. First I closed my eyes, then I used my third eye to sense any presence. I said, "I feel two beings here. Someone is standing beside me and another being is standing about six feet in front of me."

Samuel Paul said, "I am standing beside you. Who is in front of you?"

Out of nowhere, the name Babaró popped into my head and I felt a surge of happiness and smiled as I recollected the many hours I had spent under Babaró's direction in my office, writing. Babaró had been rather elusive these past few days. I wondered what he had been up to.

CHAPTER
FIFTEEN

Yesterday was a brilliant day. The sky was clear blue and the temperature had climbed to the upper eighties. Today the entire sky was a dreary gray that felt cold and damp. The wind was presenting itself in an extremely forceful way—re-arranging the patio furniture on the deck in a haphazard manner.

Because I was not from this area, I didn't know what to expect from the weather. Because of that, I questioned if I was safe.

Living in the Midwest we had prairies—the flat lands—and often we dealt with strong winds and were mindful of how quickly the wind could shift, and with that, a tornado could become a threat. Here I was dealing with mountains and canyons. *Would the canyon assist the wind somehow, creating a vortex and sweeping this house with me in it away?*

I was trying to concentrate on other things, but the wind continued to make itself known in a loud voice that was restless and at times even violent. I was kept somewhat distracted and even on edge because of the wind's unyielding persistence—the sudden unexplained noises.

One of the windowpanes was loose and was rattling—the same window the tree branch kept scratching at. The cool damp air steadily blew in.

Suddenly, there was an explosion of activity outdoors. I felt the house shake. The other side of the duplex was empty. The two sides shared a common wall, the wooden front porch, and the concrete back patio.

My place was more like a cabin because it was rustic and surrounded by sprawling mature evergreen trees, yews, other bushes, and vines that had overtaken the area, hiding the cabin from view. It is as if the cabin were located deep in the wilderness.

In reality, though, I was right next door to the owner's family and a mere mile and a half from a major highway that connected Prescott to Prescott Valley, where I could find any store that I could possibly want.

The people from the city would consider this cabin to be a bungalow or maybe a studio apartment, because it was all one comfortable room.

The place was spacious enough for me and decorated nicely with wicker furniture and antiques, with other items that made the place feel inviting and lived in. The kitchenette had a tiny countertop just big enough to have a small sink, a hotplate, and a toaster oven on. There was a microwave as well, but it was over by the window that was loose. I used an old wooden ironing board as a place for my coffee pot, utensil container, and a basket full of fresh fruit.

Another loud bang startled me, and I heard the cabin groan from the strain. The sound came from next door. I was curious, but wondered if it was safe to go outdoors and see what caused the noise.

Being preoccupied with the weather, it was impossible for me to relax with my music, so I decided to open the sliding glass door and see how strong the wind was. Okay, I hurried out the door to peak around the corner. Immediately, I saw what had made the loud commotion. The glass patio tabletop had been lifted from its green metal frame and now it rested precariously against the glass door of the adjoining unit. It was a wonder nothing broke. The wind could easily pick it up again and take it sailing to God knows where.

Quickly, I scanned the patio and saw that the lounge chair on my side had scooted several feet from its original position. The inexpensive lightweight plastic lawn chairs, that were so popular now, were scattered here and there. One chair had totally disappeared altogether.

I went back inside and quickly shut the door and shivered. Again, I surveyed the sky and wondered if this was all we were in for, or would there be something more coming?

As I moved away from the door, deeper into my cabin, I saw the old worn quilt that was folded neatly and placed on top of the antique trunk at the foot of the bed. I picked up the quilt more to sooth my nerves than for warmth and sat down to read the book that I had started yesterday, *Zen and the Art of Playing Poker.*

So far, I was impressed with it, although it seemed to be targeted for an audience who wasn't particularly highly educated. I had brought the book along in case I might have time to read it.

A few weeks ago Allen had suggested I read the book. Allen was into poker playing. He was all for going to the casino. I wanted to understand what the draw was for Allen to play poker. He loved to play the slots. Me? I am not drawn or remotely interested in this kind of pastime. However, I knew there had to be something there that kept Allen interested, and I wanted to know what it was. That was why I brought the book along and was willing to read it.

In the book, *Zen and the Art of Playing Poker,* the author wrote of going into a neutral or *zen* state of being and staying in this place when you are playing cards. The author explained that the objective is to never allow your emotions to sway your logical thinking—how you make your decisions. In essence, you are fine with whatever happens. That means if you are down $500 you have no feeling whatsoever concerning the matter. In essence, you are detached, the same being for when you are up $500. If you become attached with emotion, this will become evident with how you play your cards. (This is all fine and good. However, first you must have $500 to play with. Allen does not.)

Basically, it was a way to be in the moment. Allen was using this tool or discipline to teach himself not to let his ego take control. But was this the entire reason he was gambling? No. He was using it for his income. Gambling is a game of chance. So far I had seen absolutely no stability in this game or his "work," as Allen called it. I was not saying there never would be. I just hadn't seen it yet.

At first, I thought that maybe Allen had an addiction, and maybe he does. I just didn't know. This was part of why I was having such a difficult time with Allen. I was in judgment of his activities. I wanted security in my relationship and in my income, and yes, I realized that nothing is 100% certain.

However, he does work with his guides and is preparing himself for the shift to the fifth dimension. What I had seen was a strong dedication and solid disciplines. It was his values I questioned!

My main concern was that he didn't have a *real* income. The guides were supporting him with this way of being. This meant they were not in judgment of his choice of self-expression. But did they believe this was for the highest good? They had assured me that they do believe it is, because he is learning a lesson. Until he learns the lesson, I suspect he will stay in that situation or one very similar.

Take me, for example. I had just come out of a divorce and was afraid of having no money and no one to rely on. Dating a man who had no money was pushing every button. I went into fear when I thought of not having an income. So I had, somehow, manifested this relationship with Allen, his energy—bringing it or him directly into my reality. I do care for him and he does have many wonderful qualities.

But I questioned why on Earth I would want to be with a man who doesn't work for a steady income but gambles, instead, in hopes of winning a few dollars? Basically he was always broke, and to date he had never *taken* me out. His idea of a fun time was to go to the casino, play the slots, and eat at the buffet.

It was my opinion that our relationship, no matter how fantastic the sex was, didn't live up to my expectations. However, I could almost see the design to it. If I could relax with this relationship, it would mean that I had let go of my fear of poverty—of lack.

There was another piece to this—the issue of equality that I could trace directly back to my childhood. In some areas I had allowed myself to be taken advantage of—not treated fairly because I had felt intimidated on some level. I had been programed to stand back and let the man make up the rules. I was finding myself unable to continue to accept situations that were not for my highest good.

My belief went back to my own brother, who didn't carry his weight in certain situations. I saw the similarity between my brother and Allen. At that time in my life, I felt that I wasn't important enough in the family dynamics to be treated fairly. At least that was what I heard them say from their actions.

Possibly the guides have brought Allen and I together so I could finally resolve this issue once and for all.

Several years ago when I was raising my then teenage children, I was told that I was enabling them by doing too much for them. I was advised to never do for someone who can do for themself, as I was stealing their lessons.

Was I enabling Allen now? I mean, I paid for all of our dinners out and we always used my car, my gas. I felt cheated and used, and I resented it. Shouldn't our relationship be a partnership, to which both of us contribute monetarily? Didn't I deserve to be with a man who I respected?

Then I looked at how he was so similar to me in other ways. I was shaking my head because I really didn't know. I wanted my mate to be responsible and have a job—be secure. I wanted to know that there was someone else besides me bringing in an income.

Suddenly, I felt my vibration go higher and a pressure in my chest. I felt the love and gave thanks for those who were assisting me. I stilled myself and listened. I knew someone was here. It was probably Samuel Paul. Then I heard a man speak to me. "Nakala, you have felt a heavy burden within this relationship from the beginning. Sweetheart, this is Samuel Paul."

I shook my head in disbelief at my dilemma. Somehow I had created it. *How? Why?* I noticed the familiar tightness in my abdomen—anxiety. Wow, how on Earth did I manage to get into this situation? I am having trouble believing where I am at—the relationship I am in.

"Samuel Paul, what is it I am supposed to do here? I feel a connection to Allen, but I do not respect his line of work. I feel that since we are in the third dimension it is important to be responsible and earn our way, and that means having stability and paying our bills on time with money that we have earned in an honest manner. He has a daughter and is supposed to pay child support each month."

I wanted to go on but Samuel Paul stopped me. "Nakala, soften yourself. Allow me to teach you what it is you must know in order for you to go forward.

"Now, what I have to say will seem quite extraordinary to you. The two of you, Allen and yourself, were set to work together, revealing certain fears and then working to alleviate those fears.

"We have already established that one of your fears is going into retirement with little income. We also have established that you hold tight the fear of not being treated with respect and not being treated as an equal.

"I remind you that you are working with us and for us and you will gain notoriety and a worthy income for this service you do for humanity. You will always have what you require in this life. We will see to it.

"Sometimes in life, my dear Nakala, there are those who take care of others—possibly they are in a better position to assist financially.

"Allen has lived frugally all his adult life. His aim is to live in comfort, but not extravagance. This is how he has come to be."

Samuel Paul continued, "I can speak for him. I know his heart, Miss.

"I understand that you feel you are being taken advantage of. The proceedings from your divorce settlement were intended to be used when you are older and retired. I tell you, live for this moment!"

I understood what Samuel Paul was telling me, but at the same time, what about preparing for retirement? What about saving for a rainy day? I had seen many people who did not prepare for the future and now lived in conditions undesirable even to the point of not having enough money to make ends meet.

"Ah, remember the message you received just before you took Allen out for dinner the last time. 'Live in this moment; live in abandon.' You are here to relax and live in the faith that God provides all that you require. Know it! Go forth, my dearest Nakala."

I still felt I wasn't seeing the entire picture. I felt unsettled, like maybe I misunderstood Samuel Paul's message.

I protested. "Samuel Paul, there has to be a balance here. What about paying my bills? I must be able to pay my way! You know I do not have a steady income now. If I continue to spend money frivolously, I will have nothing left in a short time."

I felt Samuel Paul's energy shift and knew he was about to do something. Was he losing patience with me? I understood that he was saying to have faith that I will always have what I require, but I had been taught to spend my money wisely...be responsible. Lately, the money has literally flown from my checking account. Lately, there have been many major purchases.

"You do know, Samuel Paul, I have been supporting my mother and her friend, right?"

Noticing that I was holding my breath, I stopped and consciously breathed in and emptied my mind from any thought to center myself. Samuel Paul had been listening to me ramble on. "Oh, God, Samuel Paul. I am sorry. Of course you know I am supporting my mother.

"Samuel Paul, I know I have to relax, let myself go through the steps, and enjoy the journey. I have seen my guides do amazing things for me and I know that they will continue to connect me with people who will assist me in whatever way I need. I know it without a single doubt! Yet, when I am constantly giving and giving without receiving, I get really nervous. Really, I feel threatened, and on some level I resent it."

"Nakala, you are working from the root chakra, which is survival and grounding. It is the center, when balanced, which allows you to feel safe. You, Nakala, are allowing ego to step in with thoughts and feelings that are fear-based. Nakala, let go of the fear. Live in faith. Allow God to work through you for the highest good."

Samuel Paul continued, "When it comes to Allen, just understand that you have not come into alignment yet. There is a flow that is meant to occur and will if you let go of the fear. Honey, we see you when you are with him. The colors are so beautiful in your aura. We feel you. The emotions are of love."

CHAPTER
SIXTEEN

After Samuel Paul's last statement, he politely excused himself. It was time for me to get my lunch. So I got up and went to my kitchenette to consider my options and settled on some lentil soup—kind of fitting for a day like today.

Often, I wondered what the guides did when they were not working with me. Really…what do beings of light from the Pleiades do to occupy themselves?

Sometimes, in my mind's eye, I saw Nathanal sitting on the floor in the corner by himself, working with a device that looked like some type of computer. I wondered what he did when he was not talking to me.

Nathanal told me that he is a scholar. He is constantly studying and learning to adapt to new situations. I know Nathanal is an avid writer, reader, and speaker. I have seen him in action on countless occasions. He says he prays to the same God I do, for the highest good for all of creation. Nathanal says he is in gratitude always. Nathanal is highly motivated and gifted and is working his way up the ladder, just like I am. The only difference is that he is working from a higher level of consciousness.

The Pleiadians tell me they do not work with a monetary system like we do here. Why should they? They are able to and do manifest whatever they want at a level that we in our humanness cannot even begin to comprehend.

There are rumors saying that our entire economic system will be reshaped. This subject arouses my interest at a deep level. At times, I have asked my guides when that "reshaping" might happen and how it may come about. To date, I have not received any clear-cut answers.

The response I have received to my inquiry concerning the reshaping of our monetary system is there are always possibilities and probabilities, but the outcome that we will see manifested in our reality has yet to be decided. I am told what happens depends on what we, as a collective, want to happen in our reality—how focused we are in any given area. Everything is energy and everything is constantly moving. The future is always shifting.

✳ ✳ ✳

The cabin strained under the constant pressure of the wind, and it was making a strange, moaning sound. It was as if the cabin were alive and adamantly protesting to the wind pushing against it!

My anxiety level had gone up a notch. It was a short time after noon, yet the sky looked to be after sunset. As I looked out the back door over and into the canyon, I could see clouds of dirt and debris rising and swirling amongst the ragged clumps of vegetation and rocks. The sky had grown even darker—more threatening.

It didn't seem possible, but I could clearly see off to the southeast, hanging low over the top of the mountains, that the sky had taken on an even more ominous shade of gray, deep and foreboding. I knew it was raining. The temperature had dropped at least twenty degrees. I knew we were in for *it*…I just didn't know what *it* was.

My lentil soup didn't satisfy me, even though it was warm and filling. A cappuccino sure sounded good. However, in order to get a cappuccino I would have to go a few miles into town. To do that really wasn't a good idea. It was better to stay here and rest. I had come to know the pain quite well—it seemed like it wanted to make itself a place to stay; digging in deep for the long haul.

There were times when the pain was gone, but it had just taken a short break in its life. I had found there was a definite correlation to my pain and being in a sitting position. Right now, what I wanted to do most was get out and see Prescott and the surrounding areas and to write the book Samuel Paul promised, neither of which I could do and keep comfortable. So for most of the time I kept immobile and in a reclined position.

Prescott seemed to be such a nice little community. Down on the square where the courthouse was, there were lots of little shops and eateries. The town had character and a charming quality to it, but it definitely catered to the tourists.

The first weekend, when I was looking for a place to stay, I noticed several jewelry shops that I wanted to visit. Now, I wondered if that would ever happen. Just going to get groceries was more than enough for now.

Without warning, there was a loud pop in the wall. The sound no longer startled me. I knew it was either the cabin speaking or one of my guides trying to direct my attention.

I waited to see if anyone would announce themselves by tuning-in to the frequency. Really it was nothing more than setting my focus to my inner ear. Nothing happened. Then I heard another loud pop. "Okay guys," I said out loud, "Who's here?" Telepathically, I heard someone making a sound like he was clearing his throat to let me know he was in the room. I repeated my question, "Who's here?"

"Oh, I am sorry, Miss, I was listening to Nathanal. It is me, Babaró. I have come for you. We have work to do together. Get my book, please."

After I got Babaró's journal, he began. "It is time for me to explain my position—my function concerning you and this group. I have been working with you since the beginning—when you first breathed in the divine cosmic energy.

"Quem, your father and master, has given me exemplary action—reign over the goings on in your sphere. He states plainly that I am to use my discretion in all matters concerning you.

"If by happenstance I should have a question, I am to hold council—all members of Telbar are to give forth their views on subject at hand." (Telbar is a committee that works specifically with my ascension.)

"Never will I go forth without a decision that has been created out of a knowing—a love that is definitive and sound for the highest good of all! We as a whole will look at all angles and decipher what is the best choice.

"So, my dear Nakala, I will be with you, much like a fine glue adhering snugly all pieces for a safe transport into evolution—the higher spheres of light."

His words brought me so much peace and comfort. I had known of Babaró since I first began to hear the guides talk to me. He had worked with me on different articles, blogging, the last book, and many channeled messages. However, I never knew his purpose when it came to me. To have him commit to this service was indeed gratifying.

However, long ago Father Quem had told me he would always be my master teacher. So what Babaró had revealed just now took me to another place—to the other end of the spectrum. I felt an upsetting sense of loss and despair, much like the grief one feels when a loved one has passed away. *Is Quem stepping down from his role as my master? Perhaps I've worked with my father for the last time...*

Babaró didn't acknowledge my thoughts but instead veered off in an entirely different direction. "Since the beginning of this year you have had first Stephanó, then Franklin, working with you most every evening before your sleep time. You gave yourself over to them by stilling the physical body as they stimulated receptors in the brainstem.

"You did not realize until just recently that what was being done was a part of an experiment—part of evolution. Much data has been accumulated in response to your daily patterns/habits; all in accordance to the stimulation of the brainstem."

Babaró continued his dictation with such speed and clarity that I was in awe. Babaró did not pause once to think how he would deliver his message. Babaró's style of speaking was different, but not so much that I didn't understand his meaning.

"Look," he said, "I have been assigned this project months previously. What we are engaged in is a Pleiadian scientific endeavor to study and assist the human species. All in relation to self and the collective—cause and effect.

"We study your projections that are created from thought and emotion and how it all works in accordance to inner and outer communications with self and others. Be it of a human communication or of another intelligence or even another life form, it matters not, as we are focused on all aspects of human nature as it evolves as a species in the physical body and as it evolves higher in spiritual awareness.

"This is a big project for sure! I thank you for allowing us to study your case—all of the hours you have given over to us. On your lower level of consciousness you did not realize this was an endeavor to assist humanity on its course back to Source.

"So, you see the books that you write are only a portion of your purpose. You, through this service, are receiving special blessings. I am grateful that you agreed to continue forth. I am firmly set to continue our assessments of your communications with self and others.

"Part of this project is to measure how the methodology of spiritual guides is able to stimulate or motivate their counterparts into action (those in the physical bodies they work with). Our studies are to calculate what method works best to teach you about ego and how to conquer it, taking you forward on your steps in evolution. However, this is only a small portion of our research."

Babaró abruptly changed the subject by saying, "Call me." Then he directed my vision to a photograph of my middle child, my daughter. Babaró was giving me a clue. As I worked to put his true meaning to his message Babaró gave me another piece to think about: "Don't wait until you need something. Just call. I love you."

I thought Babaró was finished with his transmission, but then he said, "Yes, the second book of *When Angels Speak* will be finished. I will assist you with it. Trust."

I understood that the photo of my daughter was Babaró's way of saying to call those you love because you love them, not because you have a question or need something. The book Babaró mentioned was the book we were working on when I received the directive to travel to Arizona. The book was almost complete and I had wondered if the book would ever be finished.

CHAPTER
SEVENTEEN

The storm had died down during the night and when I woke up I noticed that the house was peaceful—quiet. I gave thanks that the wind had stopped its incessant howling.

As I moved from the bed, I couldn't help but notice my energy level—I felt really good! The first thing I did was open the lime-green drapes covering the sliding glass door, fully expecting to be greeted by sun's warm rays, of which there were none. In the distance, something caught my eye. Something was different. It took only a moment to see that there had been a delivery of sorts. In the not so far distance, the mountains peaks were now a frosty white.

Forgetting the high altitude, I was momentarily puzzled. It snowed last night? It is spring, right? However, here in the immediate area, there were no signs that we had received any moisture overnight; the patio was bone dry. I continued to scan the sky and made an educated guess that we should surely get that rain today. The clouds were hanging low, pregnant, ready to give birth at any moment. I thought about all the different varieties of vegetation here, especially the flowers, and wished that I would get to see at least a few of them bloom in the canyon before I went back east, home to Kansas.

My stomach growled, reminding me that it was time for some breakfast. Since I had been in Arizona my meals were a bit more on the simple side. For weeks I had not had the pleasure of cooked breakfast or what had become my old standby, a fruit smoothie. Instead, every morning, I sliced up fruit in a bowl, drizzled it with honey, and then sprinkled on some ground-up almonds and flax seeds. In so many ways, I had been taken back to basics.

All I had left to do was push the "on" button to brew my coffee. As a rule, I lit a candle and played some soothing music before I began my day. It was so peaceful here, and I was reminded that I was blessed to be in this space.

Before I had a chance to take a bite of my fruit, I heard the wind begin to howl again, just like the day before. Yesterday something on the roof had come loose; now there was an annoying thumping sound every time the wind blew just right.

The pain in my gut was worse when I sat, so I had been eating standing up. Not the most enjoyable thing to do. I had begun to notice that I had taken certain things for granted. I got my phone to check the temperature. These devices were so handy. My phone read that Prescott was currently 42 degrees, with an expected high of 53 today.

Today, I felt a little trapped. I was still feeling the pain. This weather felt unpredictable and I didn't feel entirely safe. Again, I wondered how well built the house was, but concluded that I had made it through yesterday so the house shouldn't cave in or fly away either. In any case, I will live.

I chided myself and looked at the bright side. I conceded that I would not be leaving this place anytime soon. I might as well use this time and these scenarios for the purpose they were intended for—to wake me up by reminding me that God is in control and will use any situation to teach me to be grateful and to love all of creation. God knows what is best for me.

After breakfast I decided to make a pot of home-made turkey chili and hunker down for the day. I turned on the 28 inch TV that sat atop an antique phonograph cabinet. Some people are so creative. Wendy had made use of items that I would not ever have imagined. Clever.

I lay down on my bed for a couple of hours. I wanted popcorn, but didn't have any. On days like these I want to just eat. My bed had become my refuge. I had surrounded myself with my things: a blanket from home, my personal journal, and my laptop. In addition, I had two books that I was currently reading there. This was *my spot.*

Good thing the bed was king size! Instead of using my laptop for writing the book Samuel Paul promised, I was using it to get my e-mail, keep connected with my friends on Facebook, and playing a computer game.

Feelings of guilt arose because I was not writing. My job was to write! The reason I was here in Arizona was to write! *I wonder if I will ever write again.* Instead, all I do is lie around, entertaining myself any way I can. I abhor computer games, yet I am playing one. I am not even good at it. I feel conflicted. *What is happening to me?*

The book *Zen and The Art of Playing Poker* lies among my things, reminding me that I must make a decision concerning my relationship with Allen.

I quit reading *Zen and The Art of Playing Poker* after I noticed the author was repeating himself. Over and over, he was saying the same thing, only in different ways. Needless to say, I had lost interest. Maybe the author was a believer in teaching through repetition, or quite possibly he just plain forgot what he already said. Before I laid the book down the last time, I learned that quite possibly Allen was using this modality to stay detached in order to win at the tables. But intuitively I felt there was more to it for Allen. I felt that he had a problem…a problem that was taking him down. Even though I cared for him, I was not about to go with him—it was time to get off the fence and make a choice. I knew that I had to move on without him and stick with my decision!

For two weeks I had been surfing the seven TV channels that I knew about. I knew there was a way to access more channels, but I hadn't figured out how yet. It was time for the handyman to come show me how to work it. If I was not going to write, I wanted some entertainment. I wanted to laugh. I *needed* to laugh.

Even though I was comfortable as I lay here on my bed among my things, a feeling rose up out of the depths of my being. I was scared. I mean I was *really* scared. My doctor, back in Kansas, said my symptoms would be gone in a week's time. It had been three weeks now, and I was no better.

Nathanal advised me to call an acupuncturist in the area to get an appointment to help with my energy level. My first appointment was in two days. Acupuncture is one of the oldest modalities of healing there is, yet in the Midwest it is fairly new. The last time I wanted an acupuncture treatment I went to a chiropractor that also did acupuncture. I was surprised that the doctor wanted to do *acupressure* first to see how I responded. I agreed, thinking he knew best. He told me to come back in two days if I wasn't any better.

In two days I was back to see him. The doctor did the acupuncture and my energy level shot right back up. I felt alive again. I sure hoped I would have that same kind of result with this doctor.

My vibration had increased. I had company. Telepathically, I heard someone asking if they could talk to me. Before I got into a conversation I wanted to know who it was. (For some reason I didn't recognize the speech pattern or the energy.)

"It is me, Nathanal. I didn't want to interrupt you, but I am concerned with the thoughts and emotions that you are creating at this time concerning your illness. The illness is a blessing. I'd like you to view it as such.

"Our group has gone into council and decided for your highest good to not encourage you to work. The reason is multifaceted, Nakala. Before your divorce you began to write in earnest. Father Quem instructed you to write down every communication you had with the beings of light (us).

"In addition, he instructed you to journal your daily steps by including what and who you were involved with and your feelings concerning them. To the letter, you have obliged us.

"But in doing this you have laid down activities that were enjoyable to you, like playing games and watching sitcoms. We have taken away your obsession—the writing—in order for you to just relax and do things that do not require your attention like the writing does."

Nathanal's words hit me hard. "We have taken away your obsession?" *Am I obsessed?* For months, all I had thought about was getting the books written so I could get them published and out to the people. *I* wanted to get *out there*. When I stopped to examine this I could see that part of the reason I wanted to complete the books was out of fear. I was writing because I think I *need* an income. I love the creative process of the written word. But I could see that my love wasn't the sole motivation for my work. *Oh, God what am I creating here?*

I suspected for quite some time that I was becoming obsessed with my work, but I figured it was fine…in fact to be obsessed was necessary to push me to the finish line.

"Nathanal, I get it. The illness *is* a blessing—a great one at that." Then I heard his comment and was appalled.

"You are digging deep to understand why you have developed this illness. You understand that the illness is born from thought and emotions—yours!

"While this is true, it isn't the *entire* truth, Nakala. You on the third dimension are enmeshed in the mass consciousness. There are miasmas or areas that hold a collective energy. Take diseases, for example, that have been born from radiation poisoning. There are people who get caught in the onslaught and suffer simply because they were there.

"Ah, if this you experience were so simple. I speak of the fear of lack. It is the collective who has created the belief and the experience out of feelings that are derived from fear.

"I'll give you another example. Take the drama that is unfolding with the life form of your honey bees. I speak of the sudden death of untold trillions of bees. What is happening is not just happening with one bee, but with thousands of colonies of bees all over the nations. We cannot limit what is occurring to just one bee or even one colony, can we? Bees are at the mercy of humans. Bees are innocent, but because they share space with humans, the bees are subject to what the humans do.

"Bees share the same space as humans do. But humans, because of ego, personality, and of course intelligence create things not just because they want to better the planet, but create things out of greed which stems from fear—the fear of lack.

"Fear comes from not remembering who you are…a child of God, who is loved beyond measure. Because you have forgotten your true essence, there are times humans do not look at what is for the highest good for the entire spectrum of life on the planet. Ego is in control here. It goes on from there. Ego takes hold and people become greedy. You mix greed with intelligence and suddenly, it all goes to hell.

"You take your particular case and yes, your thoughts and emotions that are (I use present tense because you are still creating them) fear based have created blocks in the body, slowing down the flow of divine life force. However, there is so much more that has caused your illness. The many chemicals that alter your body's cellular structure are at fault here as well. You, through the collective consciousness, have created this situation. Therefore you are a part of it, and ultimately, you suffer from it.

"I am here alongside of your brethren to assist you to shift the consciousness of man."

* * *

As I opened the drapes, I took a deep breath. A new day had been born. The clouds had gone on their way, giving the sun full reign to bless this Earth with its light and its warmth.

I was reminded of how God wants to shine His light through us. He in His majestic Holiness continues to shine His light (love), just as the sun does. But we, like the clouds, have a way of becoming heavy with energy that must be released at some point. Until we release that heavy energy we, ourselves, dim the light, keeping us from reaching our full potential and strength.

Sadness overtook me as I was reminded that the angels, ascended masters, and even our own spiritual guides work tirelessly to guide us and remind us that we too are beings of light; we too are love. And then I realized that there was nothing to be sad about! Because we are on our way! We are learning and we are changing this very moment to allow God's light to shine through us at immeasurable speed! We too are reaching our full potential as an outward expression, as we learn to love unconditionally in our human forms.

CHAPTER
EIGHTEEN

Many days passed. The wisdom of why I was brought to Arizona was slowly revealing itself. I was learning to relax—to not *do* anything that was necessarily what I'd call productive in today's society. In other words, I was not creating anything tangible—that I could touch—I was learning to just *Be*.

My daily practices were to go through my spiritual disciplines and assess my energy to see what was for my highest good. I asked if I should go into town for any reason or take a walk down into the bowels of the canyon. I incorporated mantras to assist me in remembering who I am, raising my vibration and to instill a knowing that I am worthy to receive love, not only from others but from *myself!*

Four times now I had driven into Prescott to visit the acupuncturist. You'd think with all the needles that had been stuck into my body, I would have had a dramatic shift in how I felt. Not so. But I was maintaining, and I had noticed that some days I did feel a little better. Without knowing exactly what had been going on with me physically, it was extremely difficult to relax with what I was experiencing. My guides told me to embrace this *thing*—in other words, to love it!

Time had a way of getting away from me, even though it seemed like every move I made was tedious. I had been here for over three weeks now. Another rent check would be due soon if I am to stay here for a longer period of time.

The thought of driving home was daunting and even frightening. The pain was too intense. I asked my guides over and over what I was to do to fix this thing—fix myself. Their response was to be with it and be grateful for the lessons that the illness was teaching me.

Finally, I received the message from Nathanal that we would be going home at the six-week mark! That was in ten days. I asked Nathanal if it was wise for me to make the trip. For the first time I had begun to really feel relaxed and make peace with where I was—not only with where I was staying, but with *not writing.*

Several times I had spoken with Nathanal, telling him in a logical manner that truly there was no reason I must go anywhere…there was no rush to leave this place. I had learned that I didn't have to *do* anything anymore, although I *wanted* to write and I *wanted* to be with some of my friends again. I missed my family and my home. Yes, I wanted to be home, but I was afraid to make the trip. *I am afraid of the pain. I am afraid that I am going to die.*

There, I said it. I was afraid that I had some horrible disease and I would pass from this body before I could finish my work here—my work with the Pleiadians and the other beings from the higher realms of light. I loved my life and I did not want to leave this Earth. Truly I was not ready. *Please, God, I am not ready to leave this Earth…not yet. There are so many experiences yet to be had!*

A burden of considerable proportions had been finally unleashed. I had learned that one of my greatest fears was not making something of myself—of not leaving behind a legacy. I had been beaten down to nothing. There was nowhere that I must go and there was nothing that I must do. I hadn't been able to really write for several weeks. My greatest love seemed to have been taken away from me. I felt empty inside. The creative part of me had been set aside—not fulfilled.

Yet, I experienced moments of bliss when I connected with God in prayer and when I was outdoors in nature. There were moments of joy when I kicked back and engaged in a sitcom…when I could move away from the thoughts of why I am here—my purpose—my goals.

If God wanted me to leave this sweet Earth, then let it be done. If this was the best it gets, that was okay. I have had a wonderful life. I truly have.

"Nakala," Nathanal whispered, "It is a rare occurrence when one faces the possibility of death and is able to embrace it. Missy, what I have to say is of utmost import. You have lived a life of beauty and grace. We see you embrace our directives, such as the writing of the books and the channeled readings for the people.

"We are in the midst of the great ascension of YOU! We must continue to go forward with your lessons, which *all* are for purpose to teach you to not *react* to the external and internal pressures which would misqualify energy . It is your time to gain mastery over your *Self.*

"This is *your* time to lay down your hatred and fear of not being perfect in this embodiment. That of which I speak is *your* belief, a grand illusion that you have built to protect your ego. It is *your* time to embrace God's love, for you are His child, born of His Essence, which is True Perfection and True Love.

"We are entering a time unprecedented. The number of souls consciously working on their ascension is staggering. We are most pleased that humanity is taking responsibility for their spirituality and seeking the training in order to expand into the fifth dimensional sphere of consciousness.

"There are guardians, many, who stand beside you and before you as you make your steps forward. Yes, we are most pleased that you, alongside many of our brothers and sisters, are at a level of knowing that there are many about from the higher realms able and willing to serve you as you expand your consciousness.

"You, my Nakala, are one of many who will give forth the words necessary to lead humanity—to teach those who reside in the lower spheres of light that they must ask those (us) of the higher spheres of light for assistance. You of the third dimension must make it known that you desire our radiation, which comes in many levels and forms. Above all, we seek healing for the human race, and that is the gift to remember who you are—*Children of the Light.*

"We walk with you unseen because you have ventured from your God-Selves and have grown disobedient to the ways of God. I speak of loving all that is.

"We have given you specific direction. Remember, dear Nakala, back to the first days when we came to you. Do you remember your delight?

You were so excited that you were able to communicate with us. You grew obsessive and desired not to rest from it all. Sleep grew scarce, and with it an imbalance grew to great proportions.

"I speak on these things at this time because there are others who reside in your sphere who are awakening and because even though there are those to assist them from the higher realms it is imperative that there are those who walk the Earth in physical form to assist them—to ease them into the newness of their heightened awareness. This is part of your work, to give unto the others to comfort them and to teach them to use the gifts that they are receiving for the highest good. I say unto you! With these grand gifts comes a high responsibility. The people must be taught to use these gifts properly so they may serve God Our Creator.

CHAPTER
NINETEEN

It was decided. I would rent my cabin for an additional week. I told Wendy there was a slight possibility that I may want to extend my stay even longer. I just wasn't sure yet…I would let her know.

Nevertheless, I made what I believed to be my last trip to the grocery store, planned out when I would be doing my laundry, and began to pack up my belongings. This all had to be done in small segments to ensure that I wouldn't physically overdo it. The drive home would take me a full three days.

I wanted to plan my route well in advance. Would I go home the same way I had come?

It wouldn't be long now before I drove away from these glorious mountains. I had grown accustomed to the area and this new way of living. So to leave now to rejoin my friends and family in Kansas felt bittersweet.

I felt such a mixture of emotions concerning it all. I wanted to somehow etch the image of this place before me in my mind and remember this time forever. God had truly blessed me by allowing me to have this experience. So I decided to go out and breathe in the scenery, having no particular destination in mind.

As I walked down the hill and around the corner of my cabin, I saw smack dab in the middle of the gravel parking lot Toby, the mutt that I had met on the very first day I came here. Toby was all sprawled out on his stomach, for what reason I'll never know. I couldn't see how he could possibly be comfortable lying on a bunch of rocks, but that was his business.

When I first came to look over the cabin, Toby had met me at the front door, wagging his tail in a furious manner, demanding my full attention, and of course he had worked his way into my heart.

Wendy had said Toby was a rescue dog and was still on the young side. I remember she had warned me in the very beginning that I wasn't to leave any trash on the porch or allow Toby inside the cabin, no matter how persuasive Toby was. Evidently, Wendy had had her share of cleaning up after him.

Toby is a medium-size dog and looked just like a wirehaired terrier. His coat was a rough, wiry mess of white, black, and brown hair that went every which way, that was a perfect match for his rambunctious personality.

The gravel crunched under my shoes as I walked across the parking area. Toby lifted his head to acknowledge that he had indeed heard me, but made no effort to get up and greet me. I was going to miss that mutt.

As I walked closer to Toby, I decided that I was going to take a walk down into the canyon. Usually, Toby was just too reckless for me, but today I felt like having a bit of company. Toby loved to run. Perhaps he would join me. So I headed to the path, turned to Toby, and called out to him to join me.

Toby had a mischievous glint in his brown eyes as he stood up and slowly stretched. He then proceeded to shake out the dirt from his mane. Of course he must spruce up for our adventure. So ironic that he would even bother, because this dog was one that would roll in the mud if given a chance.

As I began my descent into the canyon, it was evident that Toby was in for the excursion as if this were the very last one he would ever have. Abruptly, Toby raced passed me, almost knocking me off balance. Then he suddenly veered to the right off the path to check out something far, and for me unseen, in the distance.

Every step I took down I took with great care as I dodged rocks, brush, and cacti. One wrong step and I could slip on a loose stone and begin a slide that would take me down several feet.

For weeks now I had held my body ridged, working to shield it from any movement that would cause additional pain. Now that I was outdoors, I felt the stress in every muscle of my body.

I so wanted relief from the constant fear of hurting myself. I wanted to forget! Breathing deeply, I stopped my trek and looked out over the canyon, seeing the trees and the wild flowers that had begun to blossom. It its own unique rugged way, this place was quite beautiful.

For no reason in particular, my attention was drawn down to the Earth's soil and to all of the rocks that littered my path. Curious, I bent down to get a closer look. I was drawn to the many colors, sizes, and shapes. Even the textures varied greatly. Some were granite, some were quartz. Some rocks had flecks of pyrite in them, reflecting the light as if they were tiny stars. Most were a matrix of minerals that were unidentifiable to me.

Without any warning, Toby, who was now dripping wet, sprinted by me, nearly knocking me off my feet. Nice…he had found the stream. I had better watch out for this one or I would pay the price. Toby zigzagged across the path, first to the left, then to the right, and then abruptly came to a halt. He looked back at me with that look of his that asked, "Are you coming or not?"

Without meaning to, I yelled at him. "Toby, I am out here for a stroll, not to have a race."

Toby turned as if what I said didn't matter a lick and ran down deeper into the canyon. I looked at the legs of my khaki pants and saw the red mud from Toby's invitation. Lovely.

Since I had encouraged Toby to come along, I felt responsible for his safety. By that I meant, I thought he should stay close enough where I could keep an eye on him. However, I could clearly see that trying to coax him to do anything would be pointless.

Out of nowhere the words Nancy had spoken to me came flooding back to me. "I have to take you to Prescott. The last time you didn't make it."

Slowly, I stood up and brushed at the muddy wet spots that were sprinkled on my pants, knowing full well my effort was futile.

✳ ✳ ✳

The words, "The last time you didn't make it." reverberated in my mind. Someone was trying to tell me something here. So I decided to ask Nathanal about it. Feeling confident that Nathanal walked beside me. I asked, "Nathanal, why did Nancy feel she had to get me here *this* time?" Already my thoughts had begun to race at the implications of the statement. Obviously, this was about a past life. No answer. So I tried again.

"Nathanal, is there something you want me to know about a journey that I had been on at some point during a past life?"

Again, Nathanal didn't answer. Instead, I heard Father Quem speak. I was surprised that he was around. "Nakala, yes, there is some information that would do you well to know. Perhaps we go deeper into the canyon and talk about it. Find yourself a large stone down by the stream to lie down on for a time."

I felt Father Quem's suggestion were wise. For me to listen to him explain something as I am concentrating on dodging the rocks down a steep and narrow path certainly wasn't the smartest thing I could be doing. The largest smooth rocks were down by the stream, so I headed that way.

Off near the stream I could see Toby sniffing around a fallen tree. All of a sudden he lifted his head and turned to look straight at me. He took the stance as if he were about to take off running. I moaned and found myself muttering obscenities. It was obvious that this dog was up to something. Then he tore off toward the stream, running full speed across the water to the other side. On the bank he stood still for just a moment as he shook off the excess water. Silently, I thanked God I wasn't any closer.

Working my way to get to the edge of the stream, I dodged trees, fallen branches, thorny bushes, and waist-high grass. Toby heard my movements, then casually looked my way as if he were checking on where I was. But I suspected he was really checking to see if I was watching him. He then took off and headed straight back into the water as fast as he could. This dog seemed to be a bit of an extrovert.

Toby was acting crazy as he ran through the water yet again, and then toward me. I held my breath as he ran past me, purposely hitting me with his body, working to prod me. Then he dove toward the water again. *This dog is nuts,* I thought.

My attention was divided. I was keeping an eye on Toby, looking for a stone, and working to relieve stress. Relieving the stress wasn't working. Toby was having a grand time romping in the water. Every few seconds he would dash across the stream again as fast as he could. My question was, would he ever tire of this? He would crash through branches and rocks like they were not even there. His reckless behavior was border-line insane.

I wanted absolutely nothing to do with this. But I could see that Toby was so full of joy at being alive and having this experience in this moment that secretly I wanted to be like him; to not give a care if I got wet or muddy. I simply would like to live with true abandon.

As I walked deeper into the canyon, looking to find that one perfect stone, Toby continued to use the same unruly strategy to engage me.

Time and time again, Toby made wild passes at me, purposely getting me wet and muddy. I tried to talk to Toby about his inappropriate behavior but of course got nowhere. "Oh, I get it, Toby. I get it," I told him, "You want me to jump in the water with you." Like I was working to gain his sympathy, I moaned, "The thing is, I don't feel like running through the water."

Then I went the logical route. "Toby, I have to wash my clothes, you know, and this mud probably will stain them. Buying clothes is just a big hassle, and besides, clothes cost money! I don't want to ruin my clothes!"

Our eyes met and I saw Toby's disappointment for an instant. Then Toby was off again to splash in the water. He was just like a willful child, I thought.

I didn't see Toby again that day, although he was deep in my thoughts. Toby's objective was to have fun! Mine?... To find a bit of peace and stay clean. Wow, how did I get this way?

I saw a large black rock on the south side of the stream—a nice flat rock big enough that I could lie down on. Oh, thank you, God, for this gift. I was tired from the walk. The stone was about twenty feet away from the edge of the stream and near an outcropping of stones that formed a tall wall.

From where I stood, I couldn't see what was on the other side of the wall. *Maybe I'll check it out later,* I thought. Here in the canyon the stream-bed was all river rocks, nothing like what you would find in Kansas. In Kansas you get mud.

Since there hadn't been a sufficient rain here in some time, the riverbed was mostly dry. The stream itself was rather narrow, but still had a steady flow of water, with deep pockets of water here and there.

The flat black stone that I set my sight on was part of the stream bed and unfortunately was directly in the position to catch the afternoon sun, making it unlikely that I would be able to lie down on it at this time.

When I got near enough to the rock, I tested the surface with my fingertips and then with the flat of my hand, to see how hot it was. The rock was hot, but I could tolerate it. I sat down on the stone, a lot like I would when I entered a tub of steaming hot water for a bath. Little by little I inched myself down closer to the stone until my back rested flat against it.

The heat was intense at first, almost to the point of burning my back, but I stayed with it, allowing my body to meld with the stone. I closed my eyes and felt my body sink in deeper and accept the heat…the strength.

My mind emptied and I felt myself give over the anxiety that I had been carrying for weeks now. I had almost drifted off when I heard someone call my name.

It was Father Quem. "Nakala, honey, it is time." My mind was suddenly alert and my emotions raw and on the surface. I had completely forgotten that he wanted to talk to me, and quite frankly, I thought if I had to speak to anyone now I'd just break down and cry.

I was too tired to hide behind my manners or my inhibitions. I felt my tears begin to spill when I asked, "What more can I carry, Father? I am tired. Please allow me to rest for a moment."

His voice softened a bit with his response. "Nakala, it is time for you to let go of your troubles. Look just now at where you are. Feel where you are. Your Earth and your Sun have joined together to ease your pain. Allow them to gift you. Let them take away your sorrows. Give to them your burdens."

I felt myself surrender to the soothing rhythm of his voice and sink deep under his spell. He was taking me somewhere, I knew. There was nothing I could do about it. *There was nothing I wanted to do about it.*

I heard his voice clearly, but all of my other senses seemed to no longer be functioning. He had taken me down deep.

My breath went deep and sounded…reminded me of tide rolling in and out on the ocean beach. I relaxed. My father was speaking to me again. "Nakala, dear one, you are to listen to me. What I say is of utmost import. You remember, Nakala, that always your Higher Self is in charge of your lessons. You, on a higher level, plan what is necessary and what is for the highest good every experience on this Earth. It was you who decided to venture to this place to assist in the vibrational shifts."

I heard his words but didn't understand. In my mind I asked him, "What?"

Father Quem continued, "Under the direction of your Higher Self, your guides led you to travel to this area now named Prescott Valley, Arizona as one of your Earth lessons and ultimately to assist in the ascension of your planetary system.

"Long ago it was your heart's desire for you to travel across this country in the attempt to find great wealth with your helpmate—your husband, Jon.

"In the beginning of your journey you and Jon were beaming with anticipation, new love, and new-found freedom. You could see in your mind's eye your ultimate destination and God was smiling with His full approval, or so it seemed at first.

"After a few weeks into the journey, you took on an illness that persisted. Ultimately, the illness would consume your spirited nature and then ravish your beautiful young body. You were only twenty-four years of age.

"As the months of perilous travel and harsh conditions passed, you grew frail and emaciated. Your Jon could not give the time you required to rest. Nor could he turn back from whence you came. He had to press on. He prayed that God would give you both the strength to carry you through until you safely arrived at that special place you both had so fondly dreamt of.

"The wilderness was thick and untamed; the animals wild and unpredictable. You foraged across desserts and through the mountains. The nights were harsh, but the days were even worse. The elements were severe. It seemed you were either freezing cold or suffering from horrific heat. In order to survive, you at all times had to remain fixed and alert, or more likely than not you would be maimed or killed. Rarely did you find yourself free of torment."

In my mind, I could see the image of Jon and I with a group of others, riding in our wagons or walking constantly, working to stay comfortable. I could feel my exhaustion, the heat, and the freezing cold. I could hear the coyotes howl at night and the other wild animals foraging close to where we slept, and knew I prayed to God to keep us safe. I felt my despair.

"For all of you, sleep had become a distant treasured memory, as you had to be on guard for any type of occurrence. My words cannot touch the true courage, nor can they touch the unparalleled anguish of that journey.

"You suffered in silence, Nakala, knowing that words would be useless—a pitfall. Deep down you were beaten, your body thin and frail. You wanted Jon to lay down his demanding and obsessive vision and at least allow you to rest for just a day or two, only in his mind he couldn't. For your safety, you had to stay with the team. He had to push on as winter drew near. To be without shelter at that time would be the end to all.

"Nakala, you never reached that paradise you and Jon dreamed of. You passed from your earthly body a few weeks before Jon lay down to rest himself. You see, Jon never saw his dreamed fulfilled either. When you left the Earth, his desire to live on faded, like a rose withers without water. His hopes and dreams vanished, just as your earthly body had.

"So you see, neither of you completed your mission that lifetime.

"Your good friend, Nancy, receives communications just as you do, my child. She hears her guides give her direction. It was hers to see that you fulfilled your purpose by traveling to this specific area in Arizona to give you the opportunity to finish that life's purpose so long ago.

To hear these words caused me to pause for a few minutes and collect my thoughts. "Father Quem, why was it so important for Jon and me to get to this area, and why was it Nancy's place to escort me to Prescott?" I felt my vibration rise and knew that Father Quem was expanding his aura with the emotion of love. I felt it on a deep and sincere level.

I heard Father Quem take a deep breath and sigh. He didn't speak, but continued to send me his love. The tears began to fall down my cheeks and I wondered what he could possibly say. I wasn't sure that I wanted to hear about another one of my previous lives.

CHAPTER
TWENTY

When I first began to hear my guides speak to me, I was fascinated with it all—I wanted to know *everything* about my past lives; I asked questions deep into the night. I found that I had lived certain lives with the same people that I have relationships with in this lifetime.

During those teachings I had been shown some events that were pivotal; many were troubling to the point of being traumatizing. From the examination of those particular lives, I have been able to discern why I had held back with certain people and why I felt connected to others.

The few lifetimes that my guides chose to reveal to me were not to serve my ego but to assist me in evolving by growing stronger and becoming confident with who I am and ultimately with loving myself as God loves me.

In every one of the previous lifetimes that were studied I had been shown that my personality and what makes my heart sing were manifested in similar ways.

For instance, the parents I chose in this lifetime I chose for their values but also because of their attributes and skills. They were chosen to teach me in certain areas and to assist me on my spiritual path but also in other areas to make me a well-rounded person—to continue on with my steps forward.

I can see clearly the design to my life—the love I have for humanity, how I want to serve and how I *feel* when I do so for the highest good—with love.

In addition, in the previous lifetimes there were certain experiences that occurred that were truly horrific, and I saw how those events (how people treated me) had an impact on how I feel about myself today. It all came down to the impact outside influences have had on me. My example was what another person has said to me, about me, or done to me or for me—how I have given these things power over me—how I feel about myself. Ultimately, it was about learning and trusting God's truth, not man's.

Those life lessons given to me through examining past lives were emotionally painful and tedious, often taking several months to get through. I had to work through the information and how I felt about it before I learned to forgive not only them but me.

Even so, it was all so very interesting to see how I had carried forward particular traits to my present lifetime.

But that wasn't the entire gist of it. There were specific experiences that engrained certain beliefs that I had about myself and life in general that stood out more prominently throughout each lifetime.

I just felt like I couldn't handle any more sadness or grief concerning traumatic events (life and death tragedies). So I said to Father Quem, "I am not so sure I want to be given this lesson. I feel completely drained, and to delve into another painful past-life experience sounds…oh, I just don't want to do it."

However, in my mind—in my heart I knew that I would go through the depths of hell and sift through any information in order to understand what beliefs I had created that had caused my physical illness. My will to live remained strong—intact—and more than anything, I wanted my body to heal so I could write again!

In my mind's eye, I saw Father Quem shake his head, then smile. I wondered what he was thinking. Then I felt his love again and I knew.

"Nakala, let's get started. Before you are born into the physical body you have already decided how you want to make your mark in the world. During the time you are without the physical body, you are free of the third dimensional energies. You *see* clearly where you made errors in the previous incarnation and feel as though, if given another chance, surely you would succeed! It is in between incarnations that you feel light and invincible and you renew your vow to assist all of mankind in the upward spiral of evolution.

"Your heart leads the way. You know by how you feel when you are in alignment with your God-Self.

"When I first began to teach you…oh, you were thirsty then. No matter how many conversations we had or what the teaching, your thirst only grew. I could not seem to give you enough.

"You knew that I was your father, because you felt this as an undeniable truth in the core of your being, your heart. No, you weren't privy to any hard-core evidence or hand-written documents stating our relationship. The only thing you had to go on was how you felt. You simply knew. There are no words to convey this feeling I speak of…this knowing.

"It is so, as well, with the joining of your husband, Jon…this knowing. The two of you had a dream to begin anew in a land unseen. What a joyous dream it was, at that.

"However, your dream never materialized, Nakala. You were so close to it." He paused for a brief moment before he asked, "Why is that?"

Slowly, at first, I began to surmise what I knew or what was logical in this case. "I don't know why I got sick and couldn't finish the trip, Father. What was wrong with me, or is it even important that I know? Maybe it was karma that I died that way. Maybe I just didn't believe that I could make the trip. From what you said, it sounds like it would take a very strong person to make that trip even under perfect conditions. Obviously, I wasn't that person. From the way you described the journey, I can easily conclude that today I would not even consider this type of journey.

"Nakala, you are from the Pleiades and are by nature a traveler. The journey itself is exciting. Perhaps the destination is merely a resting point to ready yourself for the next journey.

"In those days, on this Earth, travel was extremely wearisome—dangerous. To take a trip was a test of endurance: mentally, emotionally, physically, and spiritually. Can you imagine being on a trail, exposed to the elements for weeks, possibly even months at a time, with no end in sight? There were no bathrooms to take care of your physical needs and no showers to ease the discomfort of the dirt and sweat that accumulated on your delicate bodies. On the trail you didn't have the luxury of a kitchen with a stove, refrigerator, or sink! There wasn't running water, and some days there wasn't water at all!

"There were no comfortable beds with clean sheets, thick comforters, and fluffy pillows to curl up with at night. You stunk, and so did everyone else. Even clean clothes were a luxury. The men went unshaven. Every moment of each day, you were tested to the maximum.

"When you do not give your physical body time to reboot and heal, you become out of balance. Because you are a matrix of cosmic energy, you are comprised of many bodies. When one becomes unbalanced, all suffer to some degree.

"Miss, look at where you are today. If you were to go without bathing for one day you would be thrown off kilter, as you would begin to obsess about the filth and if your presence offended another.

"Miss, on that previous trip to the west there were many circumstances out of your control, but I speak of two in particular. I speak of the seasonal cycles that bring on inclement weather and the dominant nature of your husband. Because of these, you were not allowed to rest and heal.

"During most of that trip you were in extreme discomfort and never voiced any of it. Instead, you continued forward with thoughts and feelings like, 'Why did I want to do this?' 'I can't do this.' 'Please, God, just take me.' Over and over, you pleaded with God to have mercy on you. This went on for many weeks. Your divine will to live vanished and ultimately, it was your very own thoughts and feelings that killed the physical body you had been gifted with during that lifetime.

I shook my head in disbelief. "Father Quem, really, if Jon had stopped just for a few days to let me rest, wouldn't I have been just fine?"

"Just this year, Nakala, you made the trip in a comfortable vehicle that was propelled by an engine taking you to speeds not imagined in that life with Jon. You were somewhat cushioned from the continuous jolts with inflatable tires, shock absorbers, and the finery of upholstered seats.

"In addition, you had relatively smooth highways as well. Your drive was achieved with much ease and comfort because of today's automobile, instead of by an unforgiving wooden wagon driven by foul smelling four-legged animals over land scattered with various obstacles such as fallen trees, deep gullies, ridges, boulders, and the like.

"Nakala, you made the trip in less than three-day's time! When you made the trip during the previous lifetime, it took literally months.

Father Quem continued, "During the drive you were in intense pain. What were your thoughts during this time?"

Suddenly, with clarity, I saw a common link. I had made both trips in intense pain, without stopping to get adequate rest to heal. I just kept going because I saw no other choice. My mind felt numb—frozen. My mind wanted to race ahead and I heard myself ask, "What exactly does this all mean?"

"Oh, no, not so fast, my sweet Nakala." Again Father Quem asked, "What were you thinking during the drive to Arizona?" I sucked in a breath, knowing that this was exactly why I didn't want to do this.

Father Quem wasn't going to give me anything. He was going to make me work for it by guiding me through the steps so I would understand why I have been making certain choices. I hoped that with this understanding my body would heal.

I thought back to the first day on the road, US Highway 54, going across the southern part of Kansas, then through the panhandles of first Oklahoma, then Texas. We didn't stop until we hit Tucuman, New Mexico.

The second day, in a rush, we got up from bed, repacked our things, ate breakfast, drove to the gas station to fuel up, and headed out. It was on this day that I had my crash and burn.

Going to Sedona, I don't really remember thinking about anything in particular. I do remember holding my body in a specific position to ease the discomfort I was experiencing. That in itself was extremely stressful.

Yes, I guess I was thinking, *Please, God, get me there quickly. Please, God, ease the pain.* I was working to appear as normal as possible, given the circumstances. There were times when all I could do was breathe, so I wouldn't break down and cry. For me, each moment was a huge challenge.

"Father Quem, have you ever heard the expression, 'Grin and bear it'? Clearly, that second day, I was thoroughly embarrassed for anyone to know that I had lost control. Furthermore, I didn't want to cause anyone any inconvenience. More than anything else, I wanted to not feel the movements of the car anymore."

"Nakala," Quem began, "I have a question for you. Where do you think those kind of thoughts originated? Nakala, why couldn't you say to Ann and Nancy that you were too ill to travel?"

Again, I shook my head. I tasted blood and realized I had been biting my lip.

This is one of those questions that probably have several answers. I knew I'd have to dig deep to get this one.

"Father Quem," I said, "Quite honestly, with my upbringing I am very conscious of how I use resources. Early on, as a small child, I began to exhibit traits of being an overachiever and a people pleaser. I had to accomplish things quickly and accurately. I did things people didn't expect me to do to win their favor, like clean their house or organize something for them. I am also extremely conscious of how or when I communicate with anyone.

"These are the laws according to Nakala."

- I do not ever want to bother anyone, because I would
   be wasting their time. (They have way too much to do
   right now for me. I am not important.)

- If I was using their time, I was costing them money.
   (Thou shalt not waste money. They worked hard for
   that! Again, I am not important.)

"Consequently, I have avoided making contact with certain people, for fear I am not only an inconvenience to them somehow but a user of their precious resources—money and time.

"If I did contact someone, I was taking a chance that I may be viewed as inconsiderate, someone who wasted things, or just some sort of a threat. Consequently, I wouldn't be someone you'd want around.

"Father, I see that I have believed that I wasn't important or was just plain not good enough…ever! Always, I have tried super hard to do everything perfect. In my marriage, this was the way I operated. I kept myself, the children, and the house spotless. I worked outside of the home to prove that I measured up (was equal) and could do it all. I over-compensated.

No matter how hard I tried, though, I felt like I never made the cut. Here we go again. Father Quem, I am not even sure we are still on the same subject anymore."

All Father Quem said was, "Keep going."

I took in a deep breath and began to organize my thoughts before I spoke again. "With the façade of living a perfect life that includes looking, thinking, feeling, acting, and doing everything perfectly, I am able to give myself permission to feel good about myself—that I am good and worthy of being included and even respected in some minuscule way—at least for a while, anyway—until I drop the ball somewhere, that is.

"This is way bigger, though. I look at people the same way. In the past, I have had the attitude that everyone should do their fair share—uphold their end. If they don't measure up and end up letting me down in some way, I have become, at times, resentful or even angry with them. I essence, I have judged them and will place them at a distance or avoid them altogether. The thing is, I really have not considered why they have not measured up.

"Is this the way I discern if I or other people are worthy to be accepted and loved? Because no one on this planet is going to be able to live up to the standard I have set. There is absolutely no way!"

I paused for a few moments and thought about my thirty-five-year marriage and shook my head. "I guess I have been programmed to believe a certain way—that if I produce or am productive in society, I continue on as programmed and I stay in everyone's good graces. I am worthy to be loved."

I felt like I was finally getting somewhere, and I wanted to continue until I had it figured out. "I'll go back to when we began our trip here to Arizona in March. On the second day, I knew I was too ill to go on. However, I felt I had to keep going, because I had to save face. It wasn't about what was for my highest good. It was about the fact that I could keep going—be productive by driving the miles. If I continued to produce something tangible, they could *see* that I was worthy to remain as a friend—they would continue to like me.

"I was with Nancy and Ann. It wasn't in my belief system to say, 'Hey, I shouldn't do this. I should go back or you go on without me or I should find a doctor.' Those thoughts didn't even enter into my mind—on a conscious level, I didn't realize that I even had a choice.

"In addition, one of my rules is I always finish what I begin, because if I don't I have let someone down, even to the expense of my own body! Oh, God! What am I doing here?" I paused long enough to bring in the full understanding that I had betrayed my own body before I continued on. "So in my mind, I believed that since I began the trip I had to finish it. I can't believe this. In other words, I made choices so I wouldn't inconvenience anyone at the expense of my own physical health!"

It was then that I felt the full impact of my actions. We were talking about my body—my life—and I heard Father Quem sternly say, "You required rest and medical care. You disregarded everything your body was telling you."

I had never heard Father Quem speak like that…almost as if he were upset at what I had done. I swallowed hard, but did not interrupt him.

"I am your Father. You have disregarded your body—the vehicle that carries you through each life cycle, the Temple of God—time and time again. You love yourself? No, anyone who does not stand up for what is for their highest good physically doesn't love their self.

"Ney, there are times when circumstances are special. But you, my daughter, knew you were ill, but your choice was to ignore it."

Oh, God, what Father Quem said was so true! But I remembered well my guides telling me to go on this trip. I questioned them about the guidance I was receiving. I questioned them! But in the end, I listened to them. I was tormented with the decision to come on this trip, but I felt I could not go against their directive.

I wanted to make sure I understood Father Quem's words correctly, so I worked to restate what he had said in my own words. "Father Quem, so you are telling me that I should have never come here to Arizona and that I should have stood up to my own guides and told them no? Is that what you are saying to me?"

"Daughter, the very first teaching we gave you was that your physical body is the Temple of God and you must care for it like you would a child. Would you send your young daughter across the nation in the state that you were and are in? It is your responsibility alone, and no one else's, to see that your body is cared for properly. The body is your pass to the third dimensional world and will take you on to the fifth as you continue to follow my teachings. Without the physical body, you must leave this Earth—the physical world."

The tone in Father Quem's voice was changing, becoming more severe—with more authority. I knew this was an important lesson, and I was being tested.

"I give it to you now. That first trip to Arizona, you were with child just prior to when you and Jon began your journey from the territory of Texas.

"However, your journey began long before you took Jon's hand in marriage. Your father had violently disapproved of your marriage. He wanted you to himself as his personal servant, to cook for him and keep his house. Ah, yes, you tended to the garden and the farm animals as well.

"Your father's wife, Clara, your mother, had passed when you were twelve. He, your father had grown accustomed to your care. I will not go into this any further. You get the idea well enough.

"During the first days of your journey to Arizona, which I now deem the Promised Land, you were ill; losing your meals. Honey, you were unable to keep anything down for quite some time.

"Two months into the pregnancy, you lost the babe. You never recovered physically or emotionally. You needed to process what had occurred and you required medical attention. Unfortunately, you received neither.

"Why did you not receive care? You were traveling west with many others as a team. It wasn't as if you were alone. Along the road, there were small towns that you passed through.

"However, you remained silent for several weeks, hoping that all would be forgotten and you would have a turn-around and recover. You did not want to cause a stir by being an inconvenience to your husband or to any of the others on the team. Nor did you want to cost your husband any money.

"After several weeks went by, it became obvious to you and your husband that you were not getting better. You became despondent, giving up the will to live.

"The point here being, had you spoken of your actual status, your husband, like Ann and Nancy, would have seen to it that you received medical attention. You, however, because of your programming—your very own beliefs—that it wasn't proper to burden others with your troubles, did not speak of your pain or your symptoms.

"I conclude here that your feelings of unworthiness were born much earlier than this lifetime."

My head spun as I absorbed the implications of what Father Quem was telling me.

A few minutes passed before Father Quem picked up the conversation again. "You are nearly ready to pack your car and travel back to Kansas, Nakala. How do you feel now about your up-coming travels?"

I stopped to think. "My feelings right now are of dismay. The pressure I feel is tremendous, to say the least. I feel conflicted. I want to go home, yet I know I am not well enough to make the journey. If I can get home, I can find medical assistance and stay with the same doctor if I need to.

"Here I can find a doctor, but once I get back to Kansas I'll probably have to find someone else. For me to get medical attention here in Arizona, well, from my previous experience with the medical profession…it sounds like a waste of time.

"You say that I have created this illness from my own thoughts and emotions, and this all began long ago. If I have the power to make myself sick, then I must have the power to get well. Right?

"I do not know for sure if this is totally correct or not, but isn't going to a doctor and getting medicated just like slapping on a band-aid? You know this is what the doctors do, prescribe pills. Right? Isn't this a temporary fix? If this is the truth, then why bother with going to a doctor? I want to heal entirely, not to just cover up the symptoms.

"Father Quem. what is it I must do in order to heal? Why is it that I am not getting better?" At that moment I surrendered and began to pray in earnest for help with this. "I really don't know how to fix this situation. Please help me here."

"Nakala, this is what I have to say. You have a great understanding that you have the ability to create illness, disease, and then death through your very thoughts, emotions, and actions. This is simply where you are at in this moment, here on this Earth.

"Some of you, still to this day, do not realize that you, yourselves, are creating your own reality this way.

"Your thoughts and emotions are programing your body. Your body listens to you. Control your thoughts and emotions and you shall control your body.

"For example, if you are constantly scrutinizing your body's appearance (the flaws) and/or how well it isn't functioning, you are programming it to do just that and more of the same.

"I'll give you a specific example here. Every morning you get up and get dressed, work on your hair so it looks becoming, and put on your make-up to appear more pleasing. Who are you trying to impress? Why are you doing these things? Who is it you think you must please? Are you dissatisfied with your appearance? Are you that unattractive? Do you feel your friends would take offense at your natural beauty? Must you recreate yourself every single day in order for you to feel comfortable with others?"

I interrupted him at that point and said in a condescending tone without meaning to, "You have made your point, but may I ask you, don't you get up and brush your hair? Don't you have an occasional haircut or shave? Or do you just naturally wake up with your hair lying exactly as you like?

"Wait…maybe you don't sleep, so you don't even encounter that problem. I know I pick at myself. I want to present myself in the best way possible. It seems there is always room for improvement."

Because I was embarrassed that Quem knew I didn't like my appearance, I had dipped low into anger, but didn't stop. "I understand where you are coming from. However, I believe there is more to this. We have a creative side to us and like to experiment with our looks. I bet the Pleiadian women, and men for that matter, try different hairstyles. Is this because they, too, think they must impress someone? Are you saying that I should never bathe or wash my hair or my clothes, and after I wake up just go into town or perhaps to church without a single care as to my appearance… that I am good enough just as I am?"

Father Quem sighed, and the last words that I said rang out again…Just As I AM.

"There is a song that I used to sing in church, called *Just as I Am*. I loved that song so much. When I hear the melody and lyrics of that song, my heart opens and I know not only on an emotional level but an intellectual level as well that I am good enough just as I am. I don't require one blasted thing to be changed about me for God to accept me—yet I think I have to recreate myself, like you said, to go out in public."

"Miss," Father Quem began, "it is one thing to make yourself up to express yourself artistically by changing your hairstyle and what not, and another thing entirely to feel you must change your looks because you feel you are not beautiful. Honey, your thoughts are oh, so subtle and oh, so harmful for not only for you but for all of creation, as your thoughts are released into the cosmos to join with like thoughts.

"Tomorrow morning, as you ready yourself for the day, pay close attention to what you are thinking and how you are feeling as a result of those thoughts. You shall be so very surprised!

"As it is, each morning you are telling yourself that you are not good enough to go out in public as you are. This is a constant reminder to your body that it should look different—that you aren't happy with it. This is the very truth of it.

"With this ritual, you are bringing forth the emotion of a negative nature. Your body feels this emotion and your cells react, creating discord. This discord is the skewing of the molecular structure—the symmetry of all, creating disease.

"Change your thoughts as you go about your daily ritual and give thanks for what God has given you—your physical body and so many other things as well.

"Nakala, I shall be most happy to answer your questions concerning my appearance. Yes, I do brush my hair, and so on. I do don on particular fashion for each event I attend. But I do it with gratitude, not disapproval.

"What I have revealed just barely skims the top, so to speak, concerning the Law of Attraction. There is much more to it. At this time I do not wish to go into this any further. What I'd like to say is I have told you how you create disease. What I have not said is that you create perfect health the very same way!

"The challenge is to stay in the positive with your thoughts and emotions. Understand being vigilant of all thoughts may be accomplished in the physical world. It is a matter of training yourself to be focused with the intention that you are always seeing the good in all situations and all people.

"If you allow yourself to create discord of any sort, you may become enmeshed in the energy before you realize what has occurred.

"I wish to go further to talk on your situation specifically. You have an energetic body—a template, or what some refer to as an etheric body. The thoughts that I speak on are followed by emotion. Emotion is spirit—this is the energy. The thought is what directs the energy.

"The emotion—I speak of how strongly you feel about anything. My example is the feeling that you have a flaw in your physical appearance. You are constantly concerned that someone will notice this flaw and find you unattractive. You are in judgment of yourself, creating anxiety.

"Another example I will give you is negative emotion created from the loss of a loved one. These energies are displayed in your energy field and can be read by those who are able to discern this energy.

"You on a physical level receive what your thoughts and emotions put out energetically. This is one part of how karma is played out."

I felt a shift in the energy. Out of nowhere, I heard Father Quem begin to pray.

"Heavenly Host, I ask you to assist Nakala in her forward journey to healing in entirety. Please watch over her, connect her with information that will uplift her throughout her search of God's Truth. Amen."

After a long pause, Father Quem resumed his teaching. "Miss, I know how much you desire to assist in the evolutionary process. I know your heart and how you desire to go all the way to the fifth dimensional level of consciousness to join us. I also know how easily you are taken down. I have asked a multitude of beings of light to join us to assist you throughout your steps. Please give thanks for this that we do, as gratitude creates more of the same."

The tears were streaming down my face. I knew deep within what my father asked for and has done. "Yes, I do thank you and the others who support me with guidance and for the unconditional love that is never-ending.

"Father Quem, I am ready to go back to the cabin now. Will you walk beside me?"

"Yes, my young daughter. Always."

PART
THREE

THE JOURNEY HOME

CHAPTER
TWENTY-ONE

The day began in an ordinary way—just like yesterday and the day before. I got up and went to the bathroom to take care of my physical needs and get a tall glass of water to rehydrate myself. Then I walked to light the white candle and sage that sat on the wicker glass table to welcome the angels, masters, and my guides and to give thanks for the opportunities to learn while I was here in Arizona.

I turned on my CD player, and soon music filled the cabin—it moved and uplifted me the way my prayers do. My heart swelled with gratitude and love; I felt myself going into that special place of peace and serenity.

The pain was not as strong this morning—I felt better and my mind was clear. *This is good sign.* Five days left to get the pain under control and make the drive back to Kansas. I felt optimistic that I would be well enough to make the trip.

I carefully lowered my body onto the chair—noticing all the sensations in my body, waiting to feel pain. I *listened* to my body like I would listen to a good friend who was about to say something very important. Nothing. This was good.

As I sat there, I allowed the music's power to take me higher. Soon I came to a place of complete surrender. I decided then and there to stop fighting my process and my journey. I let go of the book that I was to channel while I was here. For some time I felt that somehow this gift had been taken—stolen from me—and now…finally I felt myself surrender to the wisdom of the lesson. I am at peace. I am not in control here—God is. Maybe my time as a channel of divine writing is complete. *If I never write another word, so be it.*

I released my fears about my physical body and I chose to trust God with my healing; in that moment, I truly saw the world with a new perception—through new eyes.

I realized my choices were simple: either stay in Prescott or go home. But today I feel so much better. I feel a surge of hope. Maybe this is going to work out okay after all.

As I sat there I thought of my beautiful guides and I remembered that I was not alone; my guides walk beside me each and every day, supporting me with whatever I am going through. What a job they have!

Suddenly, my attention was drawn to the clock—it read 9:00 a.m. straight-up. I had not realized how late it was. *Ah, who cares anyway? There is nothing I have to do today.*

Then I heard a rumbling noise coming from deep within me. I felt my vibration go higher—my feet tingled to the point of being uncomfortable. "Who is here?"

Then I heard a high-pitched sound in my ears, followed by Samuel Paul's voice: "I am to spend the day with you. I wish you to write my words."

I was so happy to hear him! Cheerfully, I responded by saying, "Samuel Paul, this is truly a surprise!"

But down deep I felt a ripple of fear. I was still on high alert. Samuel Paul wanted me to write, yet we both knew that sitting was incredibly uncomfortable for me. I went into all sorts of scenarios as to what his motive might be. I decided to just come out and ask my questions. "You want me to write? Are you here to begin the book? I am not sure that I can—or should—write."

I felt a deep sadness rise up inside of me—I was still not able to write the book—the book that Samuel Paul had promised. Even though he already knew how I felt, I said, "Samuel Paul, for me to sit for any length of time becomes a little painful. I really should not sit and write. I want to heal so that I can go home."

Instead of accepting my excuse, though, Samuel Paul proposed, "You will lie on your bed there. Gather the pillows for support. You will find that you are able to stay in that position for the length of time that is required to take down my words."

I heard myself stammer and make more excuses. "Samuel Paul, I haven't eaten breakfast yet. Oh, I am not sure about this at all…" I felt the fear grow and begin to overtake me. My stomach felt like there was something foreign and unwanted inside of it.

However, I followed Samuel Paul's directive and went over to the bed, fluffed-up the pillows, and put them behind me; I put a blanket and my laptop beside me. I did not expect to find the perfect position right away.

However, as soon as I lay down, I immediately gave myself over to Samuel Paul. I felt my body and mind relax, as a gigantic wave of love swept over me. I closed my eyes and I began to breathe deeply. Each time I inhaled and exhaled, I was taken down deeper into a world where time ceased to exist—simultaneously it was as if I was suspended in the universe where I experienced nothing and everything in the exact same moment—the infinite.

I was floating in the middle of the ocean; a sense of tranquility enveloped me as I felt the gentle movement of the water underneath me—around me. I was comforted by the repetitive sound of the ocean waves moving in and out. As I felt the cool water against my skin, I completely surrendered.

I felt myself floating in the expanse of the deep sea and I saw above me the deepest blue of the night sky decorated with trillions of twinkling star-beings. I heard someone whisper my name softly, "Nakala." My name was no longer a word—it was a melody…a song.

The ocean waves carried me out deeper until I let go of the immense burden that I was carrying. The weight lifted and I rose out of the water, high into the air, floating on a blanket of nothingness. I felt my arms and legs drop as if someone were supporting the trunk of my body—carrying me. Indeed, it was Samuel Paul who supported me.

"Samuel Paul, where are we going?" I telepathically asked. I waited for his response and it was then that I finally saw his face. I recognized him from long ago; I felt his energy and his love. I realized that I have always known and loved Samuel Paul. I lifted my arms and put my hands around his neck and held him close.

His shoulder-length hair and full beard were white as snow. Full of childlike curiosity, I reached for his beard and felt the soft texture. I giggled. His smooth skin had a healthy glow to it. He didn't appear to be very old, but his energy exuded an assuredness and wisdom of someone who had weathered many years. I suddenly felt compelled to look into Samuel Paul's clear blue eyes—I was immediately drawn in and I felt his love and acceptance pour through me.

Feelings of being giddy overtook me, and I heard myself laugh at the absurdity of it all and repeated my question. "Samuel Paul, where are we going?" I really did not expect an answer from him, and I realized that I no longer cared where we went! My mind had relaxed and let go of its insatiable desire to know.

All of a sudden, I felt myself standing erect with Samuel Paul beside me (to my left) with his right arm around my waist for support. I did not feel the same—my body was light. Samuel Paul had moved his hand up to the small of my back, giving me the feeling that he would remain by my side.

As I turned to look at him, I was surprised to see his full height, his broad shoulders, and his strength. He was well over six feet tall, and the bulk of him easily comprised three of me.

I took in my surroundings and I saw that we stood upon the hilltop of an expansive city of great wealth. I could see beyond the city for miles, it seemed. In a large meadow stood an enormous geodesic dome, and I wondered what lay inside of it.

Grand buildings surrounded us—all solid stone structures. The architecture of many of the buildings had an ancient Grecian flavor to them, with massive columns, while some of structures were more geometric, with a futuristic appearance to them.

The massiveness of it all was out of my sphere of comprehension, yet everything seemed oddly familiar. Everything was well cared for, as nothing lay in ruin or seemed out of place. The sky was much like ours, only it had a pink cast to it. There were a few fluffy clouds in the sky that were deeper shades of pink.

As I studied the sky more closely, it seemed to me as if it were a backdrop or some sort of screen, or even perhaps a holographic canvas that one used to set magnificent patterns into perpetual motion using perhaps liquid gas or a dense colored vapor that had the ability to refract light into prismatic shapes. These gases or vapors undulated and floated. They beckoned me. I felt almost as if I could go inside the color itself and become one with it.

As I scanned the buildings of the city, I could detect that all of the buildings had a refractive or prismatic quality to them—just like the sky. Even the plant life was like this! I held my gaze on a tree and saw the crystalline essence within it; I noticed sparks of light and saw movement—there were millions of tiny cells all inter-connected, and working together for a grand purpose.

I turned to ask Samuel Paul a question and saw that he was studying me. As if something funny had been said, we laughed simultaneously. I felt like I was dreaming.

"Samuel Paul," I began, "the geometric light within that tree over there, is that the life force that I see?" The colors were quite extraordinary and had a depth to them—everything shimmered and glowed from within. I did not hear Samuel Paul respond, but just knew that what I saw was the life force of the tree. I shook my head in amazement and again we laughed. It was all so utterly surreal.

The city was laid out much like the cities in the United States, with streets and sidewalks, except this city was designed to stir your senses. As I strolled down the street, I truly appreciated the ambiance of my surroundings—beautiful sculptures of Gods and Goddesses, beings from the angelic and animal kingdom were placed in strategic places along the walks.

I wanted to know who these artists were who had sculpted these magnificent replicas of prominent beings.

As I continued to walk down the street, I noticed that the city had many centralized features placed in areas like intersections and courtyards. All distinct, yet each feature complemented. They were similar to our water fountains, but the substance used was something I couldn't readily identify but was similar to plasma. At first, I thought it was something akin to lava. The plasma was not contained; it flowed freely and defied gravity. The different colors of plasma rose out of the pools like liquid tongues rising up, being fed by some invisible force. I stood there, baffled at the uninterrupted flow, seemingly moving all of its own accord. After the plasma had reached a certain height, it changed its direction and began its descent, flowing gracefully back into the pools. As the plasma entered the pool it created rings of color that glowed from within.

As I watched the plasma form a ring that reverberated outward, growing in size, I was able to detect a tone that it created. As the ring grew in size, the color and the tone deepened as well. I put my ear to it and heard the hum of the plasma rings. Each ring had a specific tone to it or a distinct sound. Put together, it all sounded like a choir of angels. I could easily lose myself in this creation. The beauty took my breath away.

And then I saw them…the great walls of geodesic glass. The patterns were immense and perfect in every way; they spoke to my heart in such a way that I began to cry.

Samuel Paul pressed against me and held me closer. I felt his love and I wanted to expand this feeling. Closing my eyes, I merged with Samuel Paul's energy and soon found that I could tune in to the city's song. It was incredible—the plants and buildings were singing. Everything had a frequency, and I could hear it! Everything had a voice. All was in complete harmony. I did not want the song to stop! However, Samuel Paul shifted his body and brought me back into the present moment; I opened my eyes and saw him looking at me. He simply smiled and said, "Nakala, we have much to do. Come."

"This place…where are we, Samuel Paul?" I did not hear Samuel Paul utter a word, but in a split second I just knew: *I am home.* Feelings of familiarity and love washed over me; I knew I had been here before, many times, long ago.

There was nothing more I wanted to do other than sit at that precise moment and take everything in, but Samuel Paul seemed to be on a mission, as he was focused on our steps forward.

We continued to walk until we came upon a group of men and women. They appeared to be gathering for a meeting. As we approached the group, each member turned toward us and gave a simple nod of greeting. Each member then stepped to the side and formed a line, which created a space for us to easily pass by.

I counted eight beings, and as I looked more closely, I recognized some of their features, knowing they were of the Pleiadian race. The way they looked at me…it was as if they knew me.

Turning to look up at Samuel Paul, I saw him smile easily, his teeth white and even. A flash of pure joy spread across his face; his blue eyes radiated his emotion. Again, I just knew without a doubt that I was home. *These are the beings that have been guiding me the past five years. This is my family—the Akasie.*

I turned to the group, searching for some sort of recollection of who these beings were. But really it was Nathanal who was on my mind and it was him I longed for. I whispered to myself, "Nathanal, where are you?" as I continued to look at each of their faces for some sort of clue to who each of these beings were. They looked familiar, but I wasn't able to put a name to any of them.

I wondered if Nathanal would give himself over to me easily or make me wait. Again, I whispered, "Which one are you? Give me a sign, my Nathanal," as I searched each face for something more familiar…something I can remember—something that will give away their identity. I felt a keen stab of disappointment when I realized he was not among this group.

As I gazed at the group, a power overtook me unlike anything ever before. I knew that they loved me, because I felt it! I closed my eyes and allowed myself to expand and give love back to them. Seemingly out of nowhere, something compelled me to open my eyes—I saw that each being had raised his or her right arm and held it straight up in the air. While keeping their right arms up, they had placed their left hands over their hearts. I gasped, and my heart opened wide. The gesture signified they were honoring someone of high authority—a master. I looked at Samuel Paul, who is an ascended master, and he looked straight back at me.

Immediately, I mirrored their actions and felt a great respect for these beings of light. I looked into the eyes of each being and gave a nod— signifying a greeting. I did not see my father, Quem, or my mother, Sarah. I looked at Samuel Paul and asked, "Where are they?"

His manner indicated that he expected that very question. He merely smiled, took my hand, and said, "Come."

CHAPTER
TWENTY-TWO

As Samuel Paul took my hand and led me through the streets, I saw the enormity of the city. The buildings, the streets, were all so white…so clean! The buildings were all made of a substance that appeared to be some sort of stone—possibly granite or marble. However, this stone didn't look like any stone I had ever seen before. I took in as many of the details as I could manage, so I would remember them later. I wanted to breathe in the sights, the sounds, and even the air itself!

Suddenly, Samuel Paul stopped at the entrance of a cathedral, the likes were no comparison even to St. Peter's Basilica in The Vatican City, grand in scope; the measurement unfathomable to me.

Samuel Paul, never letting go of my hand, turned to me, saying, "Nakala take it in to your heart space. What do you feel?" The emotion of it was overwhelming. I wanted to fall down upon my knees and pray to God in gratitude for bringing back me to this place, my home. I was moved beyond words. All I could say was, "It's been such a long time, Samuel Paul."

For some time we walked through the city, where we passed temples and grand monuments until we stood on the city square of what I instinctively knew to be Myra (Meer-uh). This city's square was immense in comparison to the city squares that I have seen around the world.

Suddenly, I remembered the others and turned to see if they had followed us. I was somewhat comforted to see that they were only a few steps behind us. Samuel Paul continued to hold my hand as we walked past and around the corner to the right of a main building, with its many steps and columns. I wanted to linger and hear the history of such a grand place, but that wasn't to be (at least not for today).

Samuel Paul led us to a beautiful garden area. My focus was immediately on the plant life. The garden was filled with vast quantities of flowers and plants. I saw species of fauna and flora that existed on Earth and many that did not; the colors of the garden were luminescent and so vivid! I noticed that the flowers and greenery actually glowed! As I breathed in, I could smell the unique perfumes of the flowers as they mingled with one another.

In my mind's eye, I saw how the landscaper had expertly positioned certain plants or flowers to complement one another, first small groups, and then entire groups as a whole. For example, some plants were featured as the central attraction, standing out boldly, while others were intentionally placed to play a more passive role to blend, soften, and complement. He used the land, the buildings, and some of the plants themselves as a canvas or a back-drop to which he added more plants, fountains, arches, and walks. This created a never-ending flow of color and texture that fascinated and stimulated the senses to a depth that was literally indescribable, but yet had a feeling of being primitive.

I heard the flowers, shrubs, and trees whispering to one another and then to us. *What were they saying?* Their voices harmonized and formed an angelic symphony—it was almost too much! The sounds the plants created were so beautiful that I literally fell to my knees as I whispered, "Oh, My God."

I listened closely to a group of sweet white flowers that I knew to be the Star of Bethlehem nearby—I could hear their specific voice—their tone. *Ah, there you are, so fragile and sweet.* I looked around and tuned in to several of the other plants; I heard their individual songs. Instinctively, I felt that these plants were singing to me—for me! I knew that they were welcoming me home.

There was simply nothing like this. There were so many types of vegetation of every conceivable size, shape, and color that drew my attention, that somehow I didn't see the grand Parthenon. I call it the Parthenon because that is what it looked like.

The steps leading up to the entrance were colossal in size. I wanted to know who had designed and executed the construction of this building. It was cleverly built into the fabric of the whole design of the city.

Samuel Paul finally slowed his pace and stopped in front of the Parthenon steps; he turned to face me and let go of my hand. He instructed me to take in the energy of the building into my heart space. Instinctively, I placed my hands over my heart and breathed in deeply; I felt its majestic power before me.

Then a vision overtook me of a man with long, dark, stringy hair. He was bent over a large table, with dozens of scrolls scattered about. He was working on the design of this building. I could see him pouring over his many drawings of the building that were scattered out over his work space as he worked deep into the night. I felt his excitement for the challenge of it! And I felt his frustrations as he faced certain dilemmas. I heard his mental execution as he worked through the mathematical problems. I heard him work through measurements, all in a matter of seconds. I was in awe. I stopped and felt his love for the project…yes, he was one who had loved this creation more than perhaps anything else.

Finally, I could not take in any more. I looked at Samuel Paul and quietly asked, "Am I staying this time?" The look on Samuel Paul's face told me his answer. Sadness crept into his beautiful eyes and I knew it was not to be. Not this time.

He held out his hand for me to take. Taking his hand, I felt him squeeze it with a power—a communication that said, "I love you and I will remain by your side." He looked into my eyes and softly asked, "Are you ready to go?"

My heart was heavy; I wanted to see Nathanal. I wanted to see my parents. Samuel Paul heard my thoughts and felt my grief. He smiled and said, "Come, Nakala. I have a gift for you."

As we continued our walk down the city streets, my mood began to lift. I saw a pavilion that caught my interest. The structure looked like a smaller version of the Parthenon. As we got closer to the building,

I studied the architecture: eight marble columns on the front, supporting lateral beams that made a support system for the roof. A backdrop of an intricate lattice of greenery covered the beams that made up the roof. The columns must have stood at least twenty feet high. The vines themselves had been expertly trained to climb and spiral up each column.

We went inside the pavilion and I saw that the thick trunks of the vines had been woven together, forming diamond-shaped patterns that extended high up, forming the ceiling. From the vine-ceiling hung huge clusters of purple flowers like bunches of sweet, ripe purple grapes ready for harvest.

I instantly recognized the scent of Wisteria, as it is unmistakable and one of my favorites. The heady aroma was quickly intoxicating me, yet I was not overwhelmed by the scent as I would have been on Earth. Here, everything was in perfect harmony.

Something suddenly shifted in my awareness. Without hesitation, I let go of Samuel Paul's hand and turned to face the group. I found the one I was looking for…Tulró (Ta-ro.) He was one of the guides who had remained constant throughout my teachings. Our eyes locked and my mind reeled with memories that he had shared with me.

When I first met Tulró he introduced himself to me as Wistereé. I had grown quite fond of him as we had formed a unique bond with one another. He had made me comfortable by showing me a side to his character that most of the guides had chosen not to. He would make jokes that made me laugh. Some of his jokes were corny, and that in itself had made me smile on countless occasions. In general, he presented himself as a friend I could talk to.

One time, we were talking late in the night, like we did so often, when he began to tell me that we had spent many lifetimes together on the Earth plane. We had married and I had given him many children.

Then he began to tell me about one of his main interests, which is botany—the study of plant life. He had explained how he had experimented with many different species.

In his laboratory, using long, slender clear-glass tubes, he had taken pollen from different plants and married them, creating a new variation or new species altogether. He was using cross-pollination as one of his various methods to develop new species.

One of the specimens that he cultivated was the Wisteria vine. Because of the popularity of the plant, his peers began to call him Wistereé. The name had stuck.

For quite a while, even before Tulró had shared that story, I had called him Wistereé. Then one day he told me his given name, Tulró Akasie. Tulró had explained that he went by many names (depending on the circumstances). He requested that I continue to use the name Wistereé when I spoke to him, but for some reason I just didn't.

Before me was a ceiling, an upside down sea of purple which simply stupefied my senses. There must have been literally thousands upon thousands of clusters in there. The scent took me to a place that bordered on overwhelming, but it didn't cross it. I felt like I may become dizzy and wondered how anyone could think clearly in this place. As if someone had heard my thoughts, I felt a soft breeze freshen the air.

Purposely, I shifted my attention from the smells and listened for sounds. Off in the not so far distance I heard the relaxing sound of water in motion, like there was a water fountain or a bubbling brook some-where. I heard the sounds and looked into the corner where the Wisteria looked like a waterfall itself, flowing nearly to the floor. As I looked more closely, I could see inside or under the Wisteria bunches the clearest blue water. It was if the Wisteria had formed a cave or protective space around the water. Stunning.

Also, there was a definite humming noise above me, and as I looked more closely to identify the source, I saw the honeybees moving from one bloom to another. But as soon as I began to watch the bees I was quickly distracted by how the vines were interwoven around the beams to create a three dimensional ceiling of diamonds. There were patterns within pat-terns. If I kept looking I would see many other geometric designs—just like the flower of life. I was getting lost in this amazing design, and at that moment all I wanted to do was study it all and be with it, but I recognized that this wasn't the main reason for my visit here.

A taller man with curly, shoulder-length dark brown hair had come to stand by my side; he was patiently trying to catch my attention. I didn't remember him from the group and I didn't notice his approach, either. I took note of his boldness—how close he stood next to me. The fragrance he wore was subtle, but aroused my senses in a way that made me feel oddly uncomfortable.

My aim was to act aloof and present myself in a business-like manner. I wanted to see him without him knowing that I was watching him. Why, I have no idea.

He was not a large man, but his body was lean—strong—gorgeous.

Suddenly, without intending to, I turned to face him and looked straight into his beautiful blue eyes. I saw the depth to him. I saw his love. He whispered, "Ah, Nakala. There you are."

My heart expanded and I got all tingly. I responded, "Ah, Nathanal. I see you." He reached out for me. I didn't hesitate for one moment, but slid into his arms so perfectly. I wanted to stay there forever.

As I stood there in his arms, I felt the maleness of him. His power that he held in check. Oh, my God, I have waited for so long…I felt the sting of my tears as they spilled over and ran down my cheeks. I felt myself shudder.

Intuitively, I knew that I had to step back or I'd be a total mess. But I didn't…not just yet. I wanted to hold on to this moment and feel the sureness of him and breathe him into my being.

This is Nathanal, my personal guide who stays with me—watches over me. This is Nathanal, who I count on for everything. There were few times when he has left my side. He explained that he must prepare the way for us when we are about to go on a journey. He is making connections, he tells me, checking out the options so he can guide me for the highest good.

Never has he left me unattended. Nathanal is the one whom I have taken the vow with—always and forever I shall stay true to you.

Nathanal I know intimately. My emotional body feels him and my physical body responds energetically. But I have been separated in a sense, because I have not seen him on the Earth like I can see myself. I get flashes of what he looks like in my mind, but that is all. I am not able to feel him touch me like I would feel a person in a physical body.

Nathanal assists in my lessons; he protects me. Nathanal is my twin flame—my divine complement.

I stepped back from his embrace, took his hand. and held it to my heart. God, I love this man.

CHAPTER
TWENTY-THREE

Inside the pavilion there were at least a hundred white stone rectangular tables with individual chairs—five chairs on each side and two chairs at each end. As I stood at the entrance of the pavilion, the tables were aligned vertically. All but one of the tables were set with fine crystal goblets and dinnerware, silver cutlery, fresh cut flowers, and fine linen.

The table at the very front and middle (furthest from us) of the pavilion had been set with water goblets and napkins and a striking centerpiece that consisted of an assortment of greenery sitting low to the table, so as to not obstruct anyone's view.

At the head of that table, seated together, were two people, a man and a woman. They were too far away for me to identify who they were for sure, but I could make an educated guess. We continued to walk toward them in silence.

Little by little their features came into view and I recognized my father, Quem. My heart skipped a beat as I began to put the pieces together. The woman? The Wisteria plant? The eight guides, Samuel Paul, Father Quem. It looked to me like we were going to have some sort of celebration or banquet. Trying not to be noticed, still holding Nathanal's hand, I leaned in and whispered, "Nathanal, what is the occasion?"

Being fascinated by all of the glitz, I didn't notice right away that Nathanal hadn't answered me. When I did come back to the issue at hand, I turned to look at him and saw he too had slipped far away.

Wondering what had attracted his attention, I followed his gaze to the area in question and immediately saw what held his interest, and I sucked in a breath. Lined up in a row at the very back or stage area of the pavilion sat five dogs that looked to be Australian Shepherds, only they were much larger and their fur was pure white. Their eyes were azure blue. Perfectly still they sat, looking straight in front of them. Their white fur was so thick and luxurious that I felt a strong desire to go run my hands through it. Their manner was impressive and their beauty striking. The way they held themselves reminded me of the soldiers at the Tomb of the Unknown Soldier located at Arlington, Virginia.

Still holding my hand, Nathanal, who stood nearly a foot taller than me, turned to face me and then took my other hand. I looked up into his gentle eyes and saw the love in them. It was as if I was floating. I saw him lift both my hands to his lips and tenderly kiss first one, then the other.

I knew what he was doing, but the depth of his emotion mesmerized me in such a way…that I felt that perhaps I had died or maybe this was a dream. *This couldn't really be happening, could it?*

Nathanal looked deeply into my eyes and softly said, "Nakala, you know where you are. I am *your* Nathanal. I love you like no other. This I pledge to you."

Yes, I saw, I felt, and I knew that he held me in high esteem. Then with a great feeling Nathanal quietly murmured, "Nakala, I love you." He paused, letting the words make their mark before addressing the question I had posed earlier. Our eyes met and I wondered how I would ever be able to leave this place…him.

"Nakala, I heard your question earlier. The fact is, there is a meeting taking place for several reasons and yes, there is to be a celebration of sorts later."

I felt like a small child before Christmas. All of these clues…*I am pretty sure I am on one of the stars of the Pleiades. I am with my family. I am with my Nathanal.*

The woman who sat beside Father Quem undoubtedly was my mother, Sarah. Only on rare occasions has she spoken to me. Never have I seen her in person.

My heart swelled as I watched my Father dressed in full regalia stand and turn toward his wife, my mother, Sarah. I saw between the two of them a great display of love and respect for one another as he took her hand and assisted her to her feet.

Mother Sarah looked to be a petite woman, wearing the most magnificent white gown, trimmed in royal purple. The fabric of her gown took on the lights and colors around it and danced in a soothing but stimulating manner—*paradox it is,* I thought to myself. I could have easily lost myself in it if I had been given the time.

Mother Sarah had chosen a hairstyle that accentuated her oval face by loosely pinning up her curly tresses to the side, with curls that hung attractively around her face. Her platinum hair accented her dress and complemented Father Quem's attire. She had delicate features—her nose small and lips thin. I didn't want to appear rude but I was seeing that my physical looks were remarkably similar to hers.

After Mother Sarah stood, she hooked her hand through the crook of Father Quem's arm as they turned to address us. Father Quem began by saying, "We have brought you all here for a multitude of reasons." His gaze shifted to me as he said, "I will first answer your questions, Nakala. You are correct. This is your mother, Sarah, and you are in the Pleiades in the city of Myra—your home."

What was happening still hadn't sunk in. They must have seen the astonishment on my face and felt the array of my emotions that were at play with one another, because they both glanced at one another for a brief moment as if they wanted something from the other.

Father Quem continued, "No, you have not passed from your physical realm; you are merely taking a brief sojourn, and I expect a most pleasant one, at that."

He paused and smiled knowingly before he continued. "Your physical vehicle or body sleeps now while your etheric vehicle travels."

Father Quem shifted his body a bit as he scanned the entire group. "Now, I believe we have your complete attention. You as a group have been brought here together at this time because I want you all to hear this from me. The Telbar has been presented with an opportunity, grand. I have decided to take immediate action."

Just then he looked straight at me and I felt his commanding presence. I knew now that he was my commander and chief, and it was to him that I would answer.

Father Quem drew in a deep breath and exhaled as he casually shifted his posture, placing his arm around Sarah's waist, drawing her closer to him. I couldn't help but smile. I admired the way he openly expressed his love for her. I thought they were certainly a handsome couple.

Again, he looked at me like he expected something of me. I wondered why he kept looking at me instead of the others.

His eyes were trained on me as he spoke. "Nakala, my daughter, it is you who I depend on to execute my orders on the sphere of the third dimension."

I didn't know what orders he was referring to, but somehow he made it sound like it was up to me to make something work. I wasn't afraid, but had a knowing that when I was in my physical body this, whatever it was, may not be so easy.

"We have been offered an opportunity to serve Our God Our Creator of all things in a unique and lasting way."

He stopped just then to give us direction. "I'd like everyone to find your seats and stand behind them. Nakala, your seat is to my right. Nathanal, you will take the seat next to your Mother, please."

I did not want to let go of Nathanal's hand, even if he was just going to the other side of the table. Nathanal felt my reluctance, saw my doubt, and took my arm, pulling me closer to him as he whispered in my ear one word, "Later." He then grinned and gave me a nod. He is a sly one, my Nathanal.

As we all found our designated places. I saw that there were two seats that remained empty at the end of the table, without anyone standing behind them. Something felt unfinished; out of alignment. I waited.

Fixing my attention back on Father Quem and Mother Sarah, I waited for them to sit down or do something. They didn't. They both remained standing, silent as they waited, for what, I couldn't guess.

Trying not to be noticed, I shot a glance across the table to Nathanal. Nathanal smiled and gave me a slight nod to acknowledge my discomfort and for me to relax.

Again, I looked closely at Father Quem and Mother Sarah's faces for a hint as to what may be expected of me. However, their expressions gave nothing away.

Then a silent command came seemingly out of nowhere that told me to ready myself and go into prayer and expand my vibration with love and gratitude. I had a powerful knowing that something truly remarkable was to take place.

Immediately, as I bowed my head and placed my hands over my heart in a gesture of gratitude, I began to pray. As I did so, I was overtaken with emotion and lifted to a higher place—a higher state of being. Peace washed over me, cleansing me of all doubt and fear. My heart expanded; I thought it may burst open. I felt a bit lightheaded, even strange, and then a feeling of belonging here at this place, once again, emerged as if I had been here before, many times.

Somehow, I knew it was time. *For what?* I had absolutely no idea. Cautiously, I lifted my head and opened my eyes. My attention was drawn to the end of the table to the empty seats. There I saw two distinct brilliant white lights, but they were positioned together—overlapped like the vesica pisces (sacred geometry). The shape of each distinct energy was almost oval, but also like a human body. The glow continued to become stronger—brighter. Quickly, two beings emerged that looked to be human, still emitting a beautiful aura of light.

Everyone had turned to the beings that had appeared.

There were no questions. I just knew. The reverence I felt was palpitating and continued to build to an exquisite level that felt almost unbearable.

The beings were male and female, wearing garments of white that somehow shimmered and refracted the lights. The aura around them was rather electrifying. They both appeared to be in their late thirties, both with pure white hair.

The garments they wore indicated that this was indeed a special occasion and they most likely would be on center stage. The man was highly decorated, wearing clothing revealing his status. I didn't need to be told who these people were. Somehow, I just knew that the man was Quem's father, my Grandfather Adede.

My grandfather's pants had a metallic-looking purple braiding that ran the full length of the outside of his pants where the seam would have been. His shirt had the same purple trim on the edges of a front panel shaped similar to a shield that was attached with six gold filigree buttons. His shirt had a stand-up collar like those similar to what priests wear. On the front of the panel lay the Akasie emerald.

Grandfather Adede looked like he had just come from the barbershop newly styled—perfectly groomed. His hair wasn't long, like some of the others here. Instead, he had it neatly trimmed around his ears and neck. He did wear a beard, but it too was trimmed nicely.

Of course, the woman was my Grandmother Adrianna, and she was dressed like she was ready to go to a ball. Her dress was elegant, with a full skirt with a low-cut bodice accentuating her youthful body. Her sleeves were full-length, puffed just a bit at the shoulders, tapering to her wrists to fit snugly. I saw a gold ring on her left index finger—the gem looked to be a rather large faceted emerald.

Grandmother Adrianna's long white hair was loosely pulled back away from her face, with cascading curls that favored her left side. A decorative golden hair comb, studded with most brilliant blue sapphires, was expertly placed to complement her overall appearance. Her features were petite. She wore delicate gold filigree earrings that were long and dangly. A few tendrils of hair framed her flawless oval face. She, too, had the clearest blue eyes.

I found myself raising my right arm high into the air as I placed my left hand flat over my heart—the gesture of honor and respect. The others did the same, as we waited for them to speak or make it known what they desired of us.

These two beings, Grandfather Adede and Grandmother Adrianna, are the grand masters of the Akasie family. Meaning they are the very top. Grandfather Adede had come to speak to me a mere three times during the last five years. I have never had the pleasure of speaking to Grandmother Adrianna.

From what Father Quem had told me, Grandfather Adede had just recently stepped aside to serve in some other area and had handed over the leadership to Father Quem. Father Quem had told me that Grandfather

Adede had worked many years to prepare him for that position. What that meant, I could only guess. Father Quem had not ever mentioned to me what his mother, Grandmother Adrianna, was involved in.

It was all very mysterious. Father Quem never told me exactly what Grandfather Adede was going to do next—if he were taking another position on another star or planet. Maybe he wanted a rest from it all. From my point of view, to have the two of them present at a meeting was a treasured occasion of immense proportions.

Again, in unison, we lowered our arms and placed them by our sides, waiting for someone to speak.

As I watched Grandfather Adede and Grandmother Adrianna, I heard Father Quem's voice. I turned to give my full attention to him as he began to acknowledge his parents' arrival by giving a slight nod in their direction as he said, "Father." He paused for a moment before turning slightly to acknowledge his mother in the same manner. Then he added, "We are pleased to have you both here for this gathering."

I glanced back in the direction of Grandfather Adede and Grandmother Adrianna, waiting for someone to speak. I then glanced at Mother Sarah and saw she kept her eyes trained on the entire group. She looked relaxed, but alert and in full control. Briefly, the thought crossed my mind that she must be rather new at all of this.

All at once it hit me full force that something quite extraordinary was happening. I wanted to voice my questions out loud. I felt nervous and excited all at once. "Why are they here? Heck, why am I here? Who is it we are asked to serve?"

Samuel Paul gently touched my elbow as if to say, "Nakala, check yourself."

With that I remembered who these beings were and that they had the ability to read my thoughts.

I then glanced at Nathanal and saw that he was watching me closely as well. His silent words were very brief but to the point. "Command yourself to Be Peace and Be Still."

Doing as he directed instantly I was able to still my mind.

It was at that precise moment when Father Quem directed Samuel Paul to begin the introductions. I had my eyes on Samuel Paul when he turned to face me, looking into my eyes. Samuel Paul gently took my right hand

and declared, "Nakala, I am your Samuel Paul." With a smile, he bowed toward me, kissed the top of my hand, then let it go. Not knowing what the protocol was, I simply did a little curtsey and waited.

Samuel Paul then stepped back, allowing the next man to step closer to me. He, too, took my hand just like Samuel Paul had and declared, "I am your Babaró." Involuntarily, my left hand flew to my heart. I felt a tear slip out as I curtsied again. I thought I may lose it. Babaró…

After he stood back, a woman turned and came to me. She took my hand, kissed it, and said, "I am your Careese," and gave a little curtsey.

Feelings of being overwhelmed by emotion overtook me. Babaró had assisted me in many of the writings and channeled many messages, and Careese? I couldn't hold back. I took Careese and hugged her tight. She had stayed by my side every night while my physical body slept. She had assisted me with interpreting my dreams and did so many other things that a devoted sister would do.

These two had been with me since the beginning. *Why are they kissing my hand like this?*

Next was Dalyleh. She too approached me as the others had. Dalyleh had just recently taken over Careese's position. (Careese had taken an-other position.)

Next were my grandparents. I stepped out of my place and went to them as if on autopilot. I took Grandmother Adrianna's hand and looked deep into her eyes, searching for something to bring back a memory of our time together. She smiled and told me, "Nakala, I am your grand-mother. I watch over you always. She kissed each side of my face and took my right elbow, turning me to face my grandfather as she stepped back out of our way.

There stood my grandfather in all of his finery. I looked at him and managed to say, "Grandfather," but it came out like I was asking a ques-tion. He took my hand and held it for a few moments and I felt him. There are no words to describe what I felt, other than a great adoration.

In a hushed voice, Grandfather Adede began to speak to me as if no one else need hear his message. "Nakala, you have strength beyond your knowing. You have heard your family members say to you, 'You know not who you are.' Nakala, while serving on the Earth, such as you do, there is little recollection of your true origin and of your service on the higher realms. You are in line for the throne. Your father takes his rightful place tonight, and be it known that you, in turn, are to begin a sincere and dedicated training, as you must be ready at any moment to step up and serve in Quem's stead.

"There are many under your father's direction, as he now serves as King of Myra." Grandfather Adede then kissed me on each side of my face as Grandmother Adrianna had and smiled before he said, "Granddaughter, you are our future. On your travels, breathe and stay in the moment. Always what you do on all counts must be for the good of all of God's Creation." He stepped back, allowing me to proceed to the next person.

I recognized this man-boy, as I had been given three sketches of him and the likeness was enough for no room for error. Benjamin looked to be about six feet, five inches tall. His face full, almost round, with a pronounced chin. (His looks reminded me of Jay Leno, the late night talk show host.) Benjamin's blue eyes were closer together. His lips were full. His nose was nondescript. He wore his straight brown hair short; no longer than his jaw-line, with bangs, and clipped around his ears. I stepped to him and smiled and said, "Benjamin," as I gave him my hand. Benjamin had taught me a little about preparing gemstone elixirs. Benjamin is the scientist who created the beautiful geodesic walls.

Benjamin didn't say a word as he lightly touched his lips to the back of my hand…*Love.*

He stood back, allowing a woman with long free-flowing blond hair to meet me. She stated that her name was Kasondra. I was particularly pleased to see her, as she is Tulró's counterpart (wife). She took my hand as well, pressed her lips against it, and curtsied. I murmured, "Thank you," to her.

Beside Kasondra stood Tulró, my guide who has many faces, a master in disguise, who loved to please me with cappuccinos. He, too, took my hand and lightly kissed it and whispered, "Nakala, my lovely sister, it is you who I am to serve," as he respectfully bowed.

As Tulró made his declaration, I finally understood that these people were my family, which I loved with all of my heart. They had agreed to assist me as I went through my many lessons while living out my life on the Earth. I looked at Tulró and told him I was honored. I took his elbow and squeezed it before I allowed him to step away.

The next man in line I recognized instantly as Stephanó from the portraits that I had been gifted through a guide named Tirclé.

I stepped forward a bit and my heart warmed as Stephanó quickly introduced himself. He knew I recognized him. Unlike the others, his choice was to kiss my cheek. He lingered there and whispered, "Nakala, you look stunning tonight." I drew in a deep breath and smiled. Stephanó has been constant since the beginning.

I whispered back, "I love you, Stephanó, and thank you."

Stephanó took a step back, and there I had full view of Nathanal. He grinned at me, then bowed. As he stood, he took my hand and placed it on his chest and simply said, "Nakala, my dearest, I hold you in my heart."

My feeling at that precise moment could not be given in words of any sort. It was all too sweet and I had not experienced anything of this kind during my life on the Earth.

Nathanal knew that the group waited for him to step away. Still he stood fast, looking deep into my soul. I wanted to laugh. I wanted to cry. Instead, I smiled up at Nathanal and said, "I love you, Nathanal," and reached up to give him a hug and whispered, "Later." As I pulled away I caught the gleam in his eyes and heard him chuckle under his breath.

CHAPTER
TWENTY-FOUR

Meeting the team was a wonderful experience, although the meeting reminded me of the time I had attended a Catholic wedding. During the wedding we were constantly reciting prayers, kneeling, standing, or sitting. The people who were of that religion knew the protocol…knew the prayers. I didn't, so my main focus was on the actions of the group instead of the content…I felt awkward and out of place. I did not want to draw attention to myself.

Suddenly, the energy had shifted and there was a bustle of activity in the area of the main entrance. People were coming in carrying large silver serving trays.

Up to that time, there had been no one else besides our group in the pavilion, and all was silent except for the constant hum of the bees, the calls of the birds, the sound of running water, and our own personal exchanges.

As these people came closer I saw that yes, they were carrying dishes, silverware, and silver pitchers of beverages. Other trays were filled with an assortment of petite cakes and pastries and many different varieties of fruits. All was served in a quick and efficient manner.

There were two servers who hung back with trays as well. I could see that they had something like boxes.

As the servers finished, they lined up behind the chairs on Nathanal's side of the table and waited for their instruction.

Father Quem stood to thank them and told them that would be all for now. They in turn all bowed toward us before turning to leave.

Again, I didn't know the protocol, so I waited. Father Quem continued to stand, and he politely took Mother Sarah's hand and assisted her as she stood up. They both turned to face Grandfather Adede and Grandmother Adrianna and lifted their goblets. We all got to our feet once again. Father Quem said, "Let us make a toast to Grandfather Adede and Grandmother Adrianna for serving the Akasie for the previous reign of 400 years. Always, we love you and honor you for following your convictions and obeying God's laws. We pray that you both will find great happiness in your next line of service. In the days to follow, I promise to keep strong your legacy."

During the toast, I saw several heart-felt smiles and nods and heard the entire group call out a hearty, "Hear! Hear!"

All I could do was follow the group with their actions. The words "the previous reign of 400 years" replayed themselves over in my mind. I was astonished. 400 years?

After the group quieted, Father Quem said that he'd like us to partake in some nourishment before we got down to business.

✳ ✳ ✳

I wondered what sort of business? Obviously, the event planned was one of great importance. Was Father Quem formally taking the position as leader now, or what?

Again, I looked to Nathanal with a questioning look. In my mind I heard his directive, "Stay in the moment."

I saw that Father Quem was making a motion with his hands for us to take our seats again. As I sat down, I instinctively put my hands under me to smooth the wrinkles and felt the texture of my dress. I looked down and saw that I wasn't wearing my own clothes. Instead, I wore a gown made of iridescent white. I heard myself gasp. I was drawn in. The fabric had depth to it and drew me in under the surface. I was mesmerized as it shimmered and reflected the lights and the colors around it. Then I noticed there was an intricate design to it. I wanted to follow the threads and find the pattern. Then I saw the cloth take on the colors around it—the violet hue of the Wisteria blooms. How beautiful it was!

I raised my head and looked to find Nathanal waiting to catch my attention. I looked deeply into his eyes. He was telling me that I was beautiful and then he smiled. I wanted to laugh out loud and get up, run around the table, and hug him, but unfortunately that would have to wait.

I felt Father Quem looking at me, so I shifted in my seat a bit to look at him. He merely smiled and turned to Mother Sarah, saying, "Sarah, your daughter requires your assistance just now."

I thought, oh, that would be so nice if someone would just please take me aside and kindly explain this to me. This…this is so wonderful but this *cannot* possibly be real. Then I began to tell myself to wake up. "This has got to be a dream. This is just a dream."

Instead of waking up, though, I heard my mother's comforting voice as she began to calmly address my fears. "My dear sweet Nakala, my daughter, this is no dream. You are with us at home in our city, Myra. We have brought you here for a multitude of reasons. Your dress is a gift to you. As you moved from your physical body, you were placed in this dress, your dress."

I was left speechless. Once more, I looked down to see the style of the dress, which looked more like a free-flowing robe that a master may wear than a dress that one may wear to a celebration. With my fingertips, I lightly touched the royal purple sash that draped from my right shoulder across my heart to my waist. The detail of the embroidery work on the sash was intricate and was stitched with the very same purple floss. The design was complicated and then I saw a flash of what seemed to be similar to hieroglyphics. I did not take the time to study the patterns, the symbols or letters. Instead, I was drawn to the detail of the white fabric of the dress that I wore. There was a geometric design to it. For me, the fabric was captivating.

Mother Sarah spoke again, taking me from my thoughts. I looked up from my study into my mother's eyes as she spoke. "Nakala, for now, please rest in the knowing that you are here at home. Enjoy this time that you have been given to be with family." Once again, she smiled. I managed to thank her for her kind words before she turned toward Father Quem and nodded, signaling that she was finished speaking for now.

They both then turned to face the group once again; Father Quem took charge of the meeting. "I have called you all here to take witness of a binding contract that is about to be laid before myself and Sarah to be signed.

After we have signed the contract, it will be passed to each of you for your signature, as well.

"The opportunity that I spoke of earlier is one that comes on rare occasion, if ever at all. I have been pleased to review the contract and give forth its content to you for your discrimination and for your approval.

"The Sirian Council of Light, who you know to be esteemed members of the Galactic Federation of Freedom, has taken a significant interest in Nakala and wishes to assist her in her life's journey as scribe for Emissaries of Light, as we near the time of full disclosure and the purpose of our presence when once again we walk this sweet Earth beside our brothers and sisters knowingly.

"They approached us in the year 2009 specifically to offer Nakala, who then went by the name Jackie, the rights to publish a book of great and lasting significance. The book was described as consisting of short stories told by the Elders.

"Specifically, each elder will personally approach Nakala with their own story. Nakala will pen the stories and make the necessary adjustments in structure, and so on. There are thirteen elders included, with thirteen stories in all. The Elders have yet to be revealed to Nakala.

"This is a grand gift for not only Nakala but all of us, as we are supporting Nakala and the idea through fruition. Several planetary and star systems are to be represented in the book. The book is a marker of sorts—an alliance on many levels as testimony of our willingness to work as *One*. Be it known that each of you will be working on this endeavor in some way."

Father Quem shifted his stance to make eye contact with me before he continued. "After the book has been written, satisfying the Sirian Council of Light and the Telbar Committee, in fullness, each elder will have his or her portraits painted to be included in the book.

"The book is to be crafted in exquisite detail from beginning to end and beautifully bound in a rich hue of the council's choosing, with gold leaf inscription. All is to be monitored by this council; they will approve each step before we proceed forward. A publisher will be chosen to work with you, Nakala.

"The endeavor that I speak of may be considered highly provocative. It is a great mark of respect to be considered for this and chosen to work with this council. Each member of this group must remember his or her place during all phases of the production of this gift.

"I remind you that it is not every day that something of this magnitude is offered to us. This gift is meant for the evolution of not only the Earth-beings but those of the higher dimensions as well. It is a great honor to be asked for our expertise."

Father Quem paused long enough to take a sip of tea and to reflect on something. Then he caught my gaze and held it for a moment. He bowed his head slightly, then smiled before he made his announcement. "You, Nakala, are our chosen scribe. I ask you, my daughter, are you up for the task?"

It was then that I stood up and asked Father Quem if I may address the group. Without hesitation, Father Quem replied, "Of course," motioning for me to go ahead as he sat down.

Turning so I could make eye contact with each individual as I spoke, I began by saying, "Thank you, my dear Mother, Father, Grandmother Adrianna, Grandfather Adede, my brothers and sisters, for having me here with you. This, for me, is quite extraordinary and unexpected.

"Several years have passed since this project was first presented to me. I must say, at that time I was flattered to be asked to assist in this project and excited to be a part of the team that would produce such a grand instrument that ultimately will play a key role in evolution.

"I remember well, being told by the Sirian Council of Light that I must be free to work on their book. As I recall, at that time I was working on first volume of *When Angels Speak*. They wanted to see that book published before they would go forward on the book for the Elders. As you all know, *When Angels Speak* is completed and published.

"Clearly, I see this book for the Elders as an introduction of sorts to the people of the Earth who want to learn more about the star people. I am certain that the great masters who are to be included in this book will weave their magic throughout their narratives in such a manner that it is both entertaining and informative.

"At the time that idea was presented to me, I had a vision of how the book would look; I could see it complete in my hands and it was truly grand, with a padded leather binding and gold leaf lettering. The edging of the pages was also in gold leaf. I knew the cost to create a book of this quality and elegance would be high, but the beauty took my breath away and I knew somehow that it would come into being and would rest in the hands of the people on the Earth as a highly respected literary work.

"At that time I was overcome with gratitude with the prospect of even being considered, and I agreed fully that yes, I would be honored to take the stories and put them on the pages to complete a book that would fully satisfy the council."

Suddenly I stopped speaking, as memories of the illness I had been fighting came flooding into my mind. I wondered how I could possibly fulfill my purpose now. A deep sadness overtook me as I contemplated what words to use to explain that I could no longer do this work.

I shook my head, fighting for the proper words to convey my regret for not fulfilling my part in this endeavor. How can I step down from my true calling? I looked down from their faces and stared at my plate for a moment, working to gather the courage to tell them what I must.

"Today, my answer would be the same. Yes, I would love to do this project, as it speaks to the very core of my being." I looked at the faces of the team members. Their faces were blank—no thought or emotion was revealed. They merely waited for me to complete my say. I took a deep breath and exhaled slowly.

I went on, "However, to execute a plan of this magnitude the physical body that I use must be free of the disease that prevents me from completing the writing process. I do not know how I can possibly accept this proposal at this time. Truly, I am sorry to disappoint you. I do thank all of you and certainly I thank the Sirian Council of Light for their consideration." I then promptly sat down.

In a flash I remembered who I was with, their abilities, and their connections. I stood back up looking for direction from my father. With his hands, he made a gesture, signaling me to continue.

Looking straight at my father, I felt a power that superseded logic. "Look," fighting to keep my composure, I began, "I want to do the writing for you." I heard in my voice a deep passion being voiced that I could not deny.

"Turning to face the entire group, I then continued, "There is no doubt how I feel. I am asking that you please assist me to heal the physical body that I use so I may do this project with you."

I stood for a moment longer, waiting for anything else to surface in my mind that I thought imperative to share with the group. I searched their faces for some sort of response—some answer to what I had asked. There was nothing.

I didn't know how to feel or what to do next, so I sat down, bowed head, and placed my hands on my lap. How odd, I felt something heavy and stiff like paper in my pocket. *Why hadn't I noticed it before?*

Absently, almost as if directed from an unseen force, I reached into my pocket and took out a violet envelope with a royal purple satin ribbon around it. All outside sounds were muted as if I had been lifted from this place and gone away somewhere else to another place, another time. All of my focus was on the envelope. No one else was in the room. It was just me.

Slowly, deliberately, I untied the ribbon, letting it fall to my lap, and I opened the seal of the envelope. There was a matching violet card with my name inscribed on the front. Opening up the card, I saw it was a letter. I skipped over the contents and went to the bottom and saw my father's and mother's signatures. *What?* Going back to the top, it read:

Dearest Nakala,

You are our daughter, only. You have been told that you are being prepared for a leadership role, grand.

We know your heart, our sweet Nakala. We know your deepest love and how you desire to serve your fellow man. We know these things.

You have suffered so many lifetimes, Nakala. And yes, you suffer yet again this go-around. We have witnessed it all.

We speak not of just the discomforts and indescribable pain of the physical body that you have endured, but of the mental anguish and emotional turmoil that you have suffered as well. We have seen you go through lifetimes many, not know-ing that God always has His arm around you, dear, as we do.

After a multitude of incarnations you have come to this place of knowing and of a faith that has strengthened much.

*It is your time to serve. There is no question to this. This
group, the Telbar, has been formed to assist you on your
Earth's journey!*

Your desire is this grand, we tell you!

*You seek the healing of the physical vehicle of which you use.
So be it. It is done!*

*Let us be on our way in our service to the Holiest of Holies,
our God Almighty.*

Blessings,

Mother Sarah and Father Quem

I felt a tear slip down my cheek as I looked up to my father and then to
my mother.

He stood once again, my father, in all his glory. I looked deep into his
eyes and I was taken in by his great and immeasurable love. What he did
next surpassed all of my preconceived notions of what my father may or
may not do in a case such as this.

Father Quem reached out to me and beckoned me to approach him.
I did as he wished and he took me into his arms and held me close.
I have never felt anything so sweet. I sank deep into him and knew yes,
it is done. My physical body is healed, allowing me to continue on my
work as a writer.

Our embrace softened and we stepped back. I looked to my mother,
seeking a reassurance of sorts that would be expected and accepted if I
should approach her as well. In her eyes I saw a softness—a love for me,
and knew. I stepped to her and we held each other for a short while. I did
not want to let go of her but knew that it was time that we get back to the
business at hand.

Stepping back, I found that Father Quem was waiting for me and put
his arm around my waist. It was his way of directing me to stay there for a
few more minutes to address the group. Father Quem asked the group if
there were any questions or comments before we proceeded with the vote.
No one rose. No one spoke.

Father Quem looked at me and softly said, "Nakala, take your place, please." He then called out to one of the servers to bring his book and pen. Father Quem lifted an attractively bound dark green book from the tray, placed it on the table in front of him, and sat down. A fine gold script caught the light and I saw that it read *The Telbar*.

Father Quem placed his right hand on top of the book, as if he had great admiration for it. I wondered what was in the book that mattered so much to him.

Finally, after a few moments Father Quem opened the book and flipped through several pages before he came to what he looked for. Taking his pen, with deliberate, graceful strokes, he began to make an entry.

After he finished writing he stood and carefully made eye contact with each person seated around the table. He seemed to be studying them somehow. Then he came back to Mother Sarah. She stood up and Father Quem asked, "What say ye?"

Promptly she answered, "Yes."

Father Quem made a mark in the book.

After Mother Sarah sat back down in her seat, Father Quem looked at Nathanal as he stood. Father Quem asked the same thing, "My son, Nathanal, what say ye?"

With conviction, Nathanal firmly replied, "Yes."

Again, Father Quem made a mark in the book. This went on until each member present had had their say.

I felt this might be simply a formality. These people all knew each other's thoughts and the level of their sincerity concerning any and all commitments and projects. Did they really require all of this to be documented?

They all knew my thoughts and feelings before I had ever spoken a word.

During the vote, no one verbally opposed collaborations with the Sirian's proposal concerning the project of the book.

Again, I saw Father Quem look to each member. This time I paid close attention and saw that he was communicating with them. What were they saying to one another? I wondered if I could hear them if I listened. I quieted my mind and tuned in with my inner ear. I heard nothing.

There have been a few occasions that I have heard the Pleiadians talking between themselves. Quite honestly, it was interesting, but at the same time after a while the activity made my head hurt. Sometimes I felt that they were just revealing information to me in a different way. They have told me that everything they do is multifaceted, so I am sure there is more to their reasons for them to allow me to hear them to talk with one another.

There was movement in the room and I realized that I had been deep in thought. As best as I could, I tried to look casual as I glanced at the faces before me. Nathanal caught my eye and once again he telepathically told me to empty my mind of thought.

Then Father Quem signaled the last remaining server standing to bring him the tray. A burgundy valise lay on the silver tray and was offered to Father Quem. Father Quem took the valise with extraordinary care and laid it on the table before him.

Father Quem opened the valise with movements that indicated he had a great reverence for the contents. As he slid the beautifully inscribed binder out I could see the gold leaf lettering with an inscription that was not written in language I could read. Nonetheless, there was a definite statement of excellence being proclaimed as to the importance of the document inside.

Again, Father Quem placed his right hand on the cover of the thin binder. He paused for a few moments with his eyes closed and head bowed, almost as if he had gone into prayer. Finally, he opened the binder containing the contract, reading each page. Time seemed to be of no consequence.

From where I sat I could easily see each page as Father Quem turned them. They were thick—the edges uneven. I speculated that they were handcrafted, with the lettering hand-written—all with the utmost of care. The effect for me was breathtaking. The scribe or artist had gone to great lengths to make the pages perfect, with a quality and uniqueness that was above remarkable. He or she had used gold leaf and colored inks with varying hues, incorporating symbolism and calligraphy into the work. It was simply stunning, the whole of it. To me it was a work of art and I felt the energy—love of it and tears sprang to my eyes.

In silence, Father Quem gently shut the binder. I saw that all of his movements were done with precision like he was focused on every moment as to his thoughts and feelings as he handled the papers.

For emphasis, Father Quem lifted the binder and announced, "This is the contract sent over from the Sirian Council of Light. I have looked it over closely and see that all is in perfect order. However, I expect each of you to carefully go over the details as well before you pen your full name and the position you hold on the committee of Telbar."

I noticed that Father Quem was watching me rather closely. Suddenly he gave me a nod to hold my attention before he began to speak. "Nakala, you feel the vibration of the document—the intention of this—and know, yes, that the scribe created this with great care, his intent pure. The contract is lasting, allowing collaboration between the whole of us for the good of mankind. You are to sign your name as well after Samuel Paul and beside your name write 'scribe.'"

However, before Father Quem handed the paper over to Mother Sarah he began to speak to me again. "Nakala, this meeting is not the first one that you have attended, nor will it be the last. This meeting is merely one that you are experiencing on an expanded level of consciousness—one that you will most assuredly access when you return to your Earth body.

"My desire is that you include this meeting in the book that Samuel Paul is to assist you on. The details, Nakala, pay close attention to all." Then he took his pen and signed his name to the document, closed the binder, and handed it to Mother Sarah. Her smile, as she accepted the binder, was ever so slight.

As I waited for the contract to make its way around the table to me I began to look around and saw an enormous amount of wealth in the building. The place was built with riches that were way beyond my means or even my imagination and were meant for a people of great prosperity and influence.

The pillars themselves, what I could see of them, were highly polished and looked to be made of a veined marble. From this distance I couldn't be sure, and then there was the issue that I was not on the Earth anymore but on a star of the Pleiades…is there marble to be harvested on the Pleiades? Ah, what am I thinking? They could have harvested it from anywhere. Or perhaps there was another way to create these things that I am unfamiliar with.

The floor looked to be of the same substance, with varying hues, veins, and swirls of the colors of white, yellow, peach, salmon, grey, lavender, and black. The Wisteria's violet blooms brought out the lavender color in the floor, while the oranges and yellows contrasted, bringing balance to the color palette. The darker colors of the stone added depth and the feeling of remarkable and lasting treasure.

Each member of the Telbar, plus me, wore white, that had that same peculiar metallic sheen to it. However, each garment was unique in fashion, exhibiting a personal artistic flavor that was executed in different ways, such as how the fabric was pleated or draped over his or her body and what type of accents were used. What the fabric was made of, I couldn't even begin to guess. The fabric gave to my movements in such a way that there weren't any constrictions; it was lightweight, yet comfortable.

My aim was to take in as many details as I could without being conspicuous—I didn't want to stare and seem rude.

From my vantage point, I couldn't detect any seams in the clothing—it was as if the garments were somehow created or molded as one piece. All of the suits incorporated the use of the same type of metallic purple fabric used for the accents in the necklines, cuffs, and sashes.

I noticed that each person wore medals, somewhat like our military do. They looked to me like they probably declared their rank in the group or possibly membership to a council or councils.

Even though the garments didn't have a lot of embellishment to them, I recognized the excellence of creativity and workmanship in each garment.

Samuel Paul put the pen to the paper and signed his name. As he closed the binder, he turned to look at me. His eyes held mine steadfast as he held out the pen for me to take before he asked, "Nakala, are you ready to go forward?"

Realizing the enormity of Samuel Paul's question, I paused before I reached out to take the pen from his hand. I went back in my memory and saw how time and time again I had allowed fear of my future, of the unknown, to control me—hold me back.

I had stayed in a marriage for many years because I was fearful of venturing out and being on my own...of finally admitting that the union was nothing more than an illusion of sorts. There was status in remaining in that marriage because of the material possessions and the job title that my husband held. If I changed my position I risked everything. I was full of fear—fear of the future.

I asked myself if I really I wanted to do this project. What exactly was motivating me to go forward? Yes, it sounded exciting, and I love to write almost more than anything else. Yes, I wanted to work with the Elders and see this to publication and marketing. But more than all of those reasons, I wanted to assist others, just as I have been assisted. I wanted to give back something of value. This project was endearing to me and it spoke to my heart. But at the same time, I questioned if possibly my ego was somehow luring me to take on this project. Was my ego telling me to say yes to the project so these people may respect me a little more?

No, I didn't feel it was my ego here that was in control. I wanted to do this because God was directing me. I love to write. This is what brings me joy. Writing assists me in the healing process and it is a way for me to express myself creatively, as well as assist others on their way. I also get to meet so many unique people. Yes, I definitely wanted to be a part of this journey.

I reached out to take the pen from Samuel Paul and answered his question. "Samuel Paul, more than anything I want to do this. Yes, I am ready."

As I signed my name to the paper I felt such a sense of excitement. I then wrote the word "scribe" beside my name, as Father Quem had instructed. I slowly shut the book and laid down the pen beside it.

I had bowed my head just a bit, reflecting on what had just occurred, when without any prior warning I heard the sounds of chairs being pushed back as they slid across the floor. I looked up and saw the group standing up. What? It happened so fast that for a second I almost went into a panic. Looking first toward my mother and father then down the table, I saw that everyone was looking toward Grandfather Adede and Grandmother Adrianna. They both were standing and had picked up their goblets, holding them to their bosom.

Following suit, I picked up my goblet as I stood up. With pure admiration, Grandfather Adede gazed at his wife, Adrianna, and then he made eye contact with each one of us, lingering long enough that we felt his gratitude and love on a very personal level. He then began to speak.

"I have given over my life to the service of God's will. I remain always in that service. For so many years, I have remained steadfast to this family, the Akasie—my family. I have stood strong by you.

"During this time, as you know, Adrianna has stood by my side and supported me in this endeavor, and in this way she has supported you."

Hearing Grandfather Adede speak sent chills throughout my body. He had such a commanding presence—his voice powerful, his words articulate. I felt his love.

Grandfather Adede looked at Quem and a softness overtook him. I could see that the tears threatened to spill over as he began to speak to his son.

"Quem, my son, you are next in line to receive the crown. You have spent your entire life in the readying process by following my footsteps to learn everything I know and more.

"In turn, you have begun to work with Nakala and Nathanal by deliberately teaching them in sequential steps all that you know, so when the time comes for you to step down they will be ready for the work that they have agreed to do as well. It is a never-ending process. Always you are going forward.

"Tonight, my eldest son, you are to receive the crown to make official your leadership as King. For some time you have already been acting in this capacity. Tonight, all will take witness to this transition. All will be in celebration and will lift their glasses to you, my son!

"Sarah, I speak to you just now. To give of yourself in this manner takes much inner strength, inner knowing, and inner peace. Oft times your Quem will be in deliberation with others. You know this. You as Queen hold particular responsibilities as well, and you have learned your role well, my daughter. We are all most pleased with the union between you and Quem and your decision to go forward as Queen. Tonight all are to take witness as you accept the title and crown as well. Tonight all will lift their glasses to you, my daughter!

"Today this group has gathered for many reasons. The first being to go forward with the committee Telbar, with the intention to work as One with Beings of Light from other realms to bring forth avenues for evolutionary purposes.

"In our hearts this means to assist those in the awakening who long ago grew to believe they were separated from God and forgot their true essence—love. We do this in numerous ways—the written word is merely one target.

"We are masters—teachers desiring to give forth our wisdom, all of us, to the masses. However, I say, we are students as well, who continue to thirst to attain higher levels of enlightenment.

"Always, we are to be open to receiving God's abundance that comes to us in a multitude of ways. Remember, we are children of God and we will always be learning as we make our way throughout our walk. We are to remember that we are to shine our light, always and everywhere.

"I have overseen your many endeavors throughout the years, and I am most pleased with you all."

I was watching Grandfather Adede closely and listening intently to every word. My mind swirled with what was happening. Tonight the coronation was to be made. I thought the signing of the contract was huge. But now…

Grandfather Adede obviously was skilled as an orator, but I saw clearly he spoke from his heart—emotion emanated from his being. His aura danced, growing brighter.

Grandfather stopped his speech and looked at me. I felt he was searching for something from me. Then, without speaking, he shifted his eyes to look at Nathanal. He then lifted his goblet toward the whole of us and said, "To Nakala, who has sacrificed herself in service to those of the Earth. We thank you for this gift!"

Everyone lifted their goblets, saying, "Hear! Hear!"

Then Grandfather said, "To Nathanal, who has given over his days, as well, in service. To a job well done!" Again the group sang out a hearty, "Hear! Hear!"

CHAPTER
TWENTY-FIVE

I had been in a deep sleep, but a sound had abruptly woken me—a noise that was unfamiliar, yet unmistakable. My heart felt as if it were about to explode, the pounding was so loud…the blood coursing through my body overtaking my senses. Someone was here—in my room. I heard the floor creak as if there were someone of significant bulk walking near my bed.

My eyes were still shut, my mind sharp—alert. *Who was here?* I dared not move. I waited for another sound. Nothing. I heard the faraway cry of a hawk, then the familiar scratching at the window, and I knew it was over. The images of Myra flashed in my mind, and then I realized that I was back in my body, lying on the bed in the cabin in Arizona.

Clearly, I saw myself walking down the streets of Myra again as if I were there. I felt the beauty of it all. A tear slipped down and fell on my pillow. I felt raw, powerless. My heart ached. The joy of having seen them and talked with them…It was all gone. Now I was alone.

Was it all just a dream? Then I remembered what woke me up and I slowly opened my eyes. Who was here? No longer did I have on that beautiful white gown that shimmered and danced under the lights. No longer was I with my father or my mother…my Nathanal. They were all gone. The feelings of separation sunk in deep and the tears began to flow. I heard myself cry out in utter despair at having lost my family again.

I heard Samuel Paul call my name ever so softly. I felt cheated—alone. "Really, Samuel Paul," I said, "Why did you take me to Myra and show me...oh, my God. You took me with you and showed me my home. I was with my family at last. I wanted to stay there! The celebration? Why didn't I get to stay for that? It was real, right? Samuel Paul, what I saw and felt was real, right?"

Samuel Paul channeled a few deep breaths through me until I was calm enough to hear what he had to say. But before he could begin to speak, the sobs broke loose once again. I felt small, insignificant, exposed, and terribly vulnerable—utterly lost.

I remembered the sounds of the floorboard groaning that had awoken me, startled me.

Samuel Paul's tone had taken on a formality, as he gave me a directive. "Nakala, listen to me carefully. I took you home to Myra, which is our city. Our family, the Akasie, resides there. For millions of years we have called this sacred place our home. You first took physical form on the land of Myra.

"I took you home for reasons many: We desire for you to write about this place to give forth the love that we send through you. We also desire that you remember your homeland, who you are, and your beginnings as a member of the Pleiadian peoples.

"I give this to you as a grand gift to take and share with the people of Earth—that we are about and always have been, in some way, in order to assist you on your journey to freedom."

CONCLUSION

It has been many days since that poignant meeting in the city of Myra with my Pleiadian family, giving me time to fully contemplate my travels to Arizona and what occurred while I was there.

As my guides promised, I have completely healed and have gone on to fulfill my agreement by writing the series of books, *The Accounts of a Pleiadian Traveler* with the Beings of Light.

By traveling to Arizona, my Pleiadian father, Quem and the Telbar used the opportunity to remind me that my physical body is meant to carry me throughout this life's experience and I am responsible for it. Throughout my journey Quem reiterates I am worthy to be loved and to love myself!

Above all, they reminded me to go within and remember that I have inner peace, inner strength and inner knowing. I always have access to these intrinsic qualities in me. To go forward, I am to listen to my inner self—my heart in all situations.

INDEX OF CHARACTERS

The **Akasie** [AH-KA-SEE] is a family surname who originates in the Kingdom of Myra, the Pleiades star system.

Grandfather Adede Akasie: Patriarch of the Akasie Family–The Kingdom of Myra.

Grandmother Adrianna Balise: Matriarch of the Akasie Family–The Kingdom of Myra.

Father Quem [KW-AH-M] **Monteró Akasie:** Husband to Sarah, son of Grandfather Adede and Grandmother Adrianna, King of Myra, Member of Pleiadian Council of Light and numerous other councils. *Quem means to venture forth and to begin anew.*

Mother Sarah Sebise Akasie: Wife to Quem, daughter of Cathryn Delenni and Nepal Sebise, Queen of Myra, Member of the Pleiadian Council of Light.

Nathanal [NUH-THAN-AL] **Sebise Akasie:** Son to Quem and Sarah. Twin flame and guide to Nakala, Member of Telbar.

Samuel Paul Akasie: Ascended Master, member of the Pleiadian Council of Light, Comterous and Telbar, Master Walk-In to Nakala.

Babaró [bar-bare-o] **Akasie:** Brother to Quem, Master Guardian, writer and guide to Nakala, overseer of the Comterous and Telbar. Last incarnation was Henry Wadsworth Longfellow 1807-1882.

Stephanó Francisco Akasie: Brother to Quem, Ascended Master, Scientist, medical doctor and Surgeon, Member of Telbar and Pleiadian Council of Light.

Caressé Pamilla Akasie: Sister to Quem, Member of Telbar, guide to Nakala.

Tulró Akasie AKA Wistereé Akasie: Son to Quem and Sarah

Kasondra: Tulró's wife, Member of Telbar.

Benjamin Kase Akasie: Member of Telbar, Scientist

Dalyleh: Guide

Nakala Maria Angelic Akasie: AKA Cathryn Sebise Akasie, Jackie Mullinax: Daughter to Quem and Sarah, twin flame to Nathanal, conscious channel, Pleiadian Messenger and scribe for the Comterous

Comterous is a large group formed to expedite the creations of certain types of media to enlighten the people who reside on the Earth in third-dimensional form. The Comterous is in charge of the written material that is channeled by Nakala.

The **Telbar** team is a committee created for the ascension of Nakala Akasie.

PREVIEW THE NEXT BOOK IN
The Accounts of a Pleiadian Traveler

In the next edition of *The Accounts of a Pleiadian Traveler: In the Light of Day. Babaró*, Nakala's spiritual master, orchestrates a meeting with her brother, David who passed on over ten years ago.

Even though Nakala is a conscious channel and Pleiadian Messenger, to meet (face to face and in public) with her deceased brother fills her with suspicion and dread. Why did Babaró want to bring them together?

Shortly, after her return home from Arizona, Nakala's guides instruct her first to travel to Brazil for a short respite at the John of God compound and then to travel to Mt. Shasta, California.

While visiting Mt. Shasta, Nakala clearly hears the message, "It is time to come home." Nakala takes the message literally feeling deeply in her heart that she must follow this guidance even though it means being uprooted once again; leaving behind her closest family and friends.

In addition, many life-lessons are woven into the fabric of the prose by many Pleiadian Masters including Adama, the High Priest of the legendary Lemurian city of Telos.

Throughout the book, the Pleiadians continue to spoon-feed Nakala secrets that are energetically encoded defying third-dimensional logic but nonetheless taking Nakala further in her understanding of not only her spiritual purpose here but theirs, as well.

www.ingramcontent.com/pod-product-compliance
Lightning Source LLC
Chambersburg PA
CBHW070948180726
48291CB00004B/1195